D1570434

SPECIAL MESSAGE TO READERS

This book is published under the auspices of

THE ULVERSCROFT FOUNDATION

(registered charity No. 264873 UK)

Established in 1972 to provide funds for research, diagnosis and treatment of eye diseases. Examples of contributions made are: —

A new Children's Assessment Unit at Moorfield's Hospital, London.

•

Twin operating theatres at the Western Ophthalmic Hospital, London.

•

A Chair of Ophthalmology at the University of Leicester.

•

The establishment of a Royal Australian College of Ophthalmologists "Fellowship".

You can help further the work of the Foundation by making a donation or leaving a legacy. Every contribution, no matter how small, is received with gratitude. Please write for details to:

**THE ULVERSCROFT FOUNDATION,
The Green, Bradgate Road, Anstey,
Leicester LE7 7FU, England.
Telephone: (0116) 236 4325**

**In Australia write to:
THE ULVERSCROFT FOUNDATION,
c/o The Royal Australian College of
Ophthalmologists,
27, Commonwealth Street, Sydney,
N.S.W. 2010.**

SUNDANCE: SILENT ENEMY
John Benteen

A lone crazed Cheyenne was on a personal war path. They needed to pit one man against one crazed Indian. That man was Sundance.

LASSITER
Jack Slade

Lassiter wasn't the
listen to reason. Cro
he'll hold a grudge fo
— if he let you live

LAST STAGE TO
Barry C

Jeff Carter, tough
gambler, now had
ranch that kept h
gunfights and card
Sturvesant of Wells
up.

HELL RIDERS
Steve Mensing

Wade Walker's kid brother, Duane, was locked up in the Silver City jail facing a rope at dawn. Wade was a ruthless outlaw, but he was smart, and he had vowed to have his brother out of jail before morning!

DESERT OF THE DAMNED
Nelson Nye

The law was after him for the murder of a marshal — a murder he didn't commit. Breen was after him for revenge — and Breen wouldn't stop at anything . . . blackmail, a frameup . . . or murder.

DAY OF THE COMANCHEROS
Steven C. Lawrence

Their very name struck terror into men's hearts — the Comancheros, a savage army of cutthroats who swept across Texas, leaving behind a bloodstained trail of robbery and murder.

FARGO: PANAMA GOLD
John Benteen

With foreign money behind him, Buckner was going to destroy the Panama Canal before it could be completed. Fargo's job was to stop Buckner.

FARGO: THE SHARPSHOOTERS
John Benteen

The Canfield clan, thirty strong were raising hell in Texas. Fargo was tough enough to hold his own against the whole clan.

PISTOL LAW
Paul Evan Lehman

Lance Jones came back to Mustang for just one thing — revenge! Revenge on the people who had him thrown in jail.

FARGO: MASSACRE RIVER
John Benteen

The ambushers up ahead had now blocked the road. Fargo's convoy was a jumble, a perfect target for the insurgents' weapons!

SUNDANCE: DEATH IN THE LAVA
John Benteen

The Modoc's captured the wagon train and its cargo of gold. But now the halfbreed they called Sundance was going after it . . .

HARSH RECKONING
Phil Ketchum

Five years of keeping himself alive in a brutal prison had made Brand tough and careless about who he gunned down . . .

BRETT RANDALL, GAMBLER
E. B. Mann

Larry Day had the choice of running away from the law or of assuming a dead man's place. No matter what he decided he was bound to end up dead.

THE GUNSHARP
William R. Cox

The Eggerleys weren't very smart. They trained their sights on Will Carney and Arizona's biggest blood bath began.

THE DEPUTY OF SAN RIANO
Lawrence A. Keating and
Al. P. Nelson

When a man fell dead from his horse, Ed Grant was spotted riding away from the scene. The deputy sheriff rode out after him and came up against everything from gunfire to dynamite.

ARIZONA DRIFTERS
W. C. Tuttle

When drifting Dutton and Lonnie Steelman decide to become partners they find that they have a common enemy in the formidable Thurston brothers.

TOMBSTONE
Matt Braun

Wells Fargo paid Luke Starbuck to outgun the silver-thieving stagecoach gang at Tombstone. Before long Luke can see the only thing bearing fruit in this eldorado will be the gallows tree.

HIGH BORDER RIDERS
Lee Floren

Buckshot McKee and Tortilla Joe cut the trail of a border tough who was running Mexican beef into Texas. They stopped the smuggler in his tracks.

FIGHTING RAMROD
Charles N. Heckelmann

Most men would have cut their losses, but Frazer counted the bullets in his guns and said he'd soak the range in blood before he'd give up another inch of what was his.

LONE GUN
Eric Allen

Smoke Blackbird had been away too long. The Lequires had seized the Blackbird farm, forcing the Indians and settlers off, and no one seemed willing to fight! He had to fight alone.

THE THIRD RIDER
Barry Cord

Mel Rawlins wasn't going to let anything stand in his way. His father was murdered, his two brothers gone. Now Mel rode for vengeance.

COMANCHE CAPTIVE

Sole survivor of a stagecoach massacre in the wilds of west Texas, New Orleans belle Evelyn Carlisle is in constant danger as a Comanche captive. Determined to rescue his fiancée, rancher Travis Dixon begins a relentless pursuit. He reluctantly teams up with the larcenous Waller brothers to reach the dreaded Valley of Tears. There he must not only save Evelyn, but halt a Mexican bandit's crazed scheme to wrest Texas from the newly reunited Union.

#️ 36099191

new
15.99

SS
W

JAMES GORDON WHITE

◆

COMANCHE
CAPTIVE

Complete and Unabridged

LINFORD
Leicester

East Baton Rouge Parish Library
Baton Rouge, Louisiana

First published in Great Britain in 1995 by
Robert Hale Limited
London

First Linford Edition
published 1996
by arrangement with
Robert Hale Limited
London

The right of James Gordon White to be
identified as the author of this work has been
asserted by him in accordance with the
Copyright, Designs and Patents Act, 1988

Copyright © 1995 by James Gordon White
All rights reserved

British Library CIP Data

White, James Gordon
 Comanche captive.—Large print ed.—
Linford western library
 1. American fiction—20th century
 2. Large type books
 I. Title
 813.5'4 [F]

 ISBN 0-7089-7953-X

Published by
F. A. Thorpe (Publishing) Ltd.
Anstey, Leicestershire

Set by Words & Graphics Ltd.
Anstey, Leicestershire
Printed and bound in Great Britain by
T. J. Press (Padstow) Ltd., Padstow, Cornwall

This book is printed on acid-free paper

To my wife Marie
for her unwavering love and
belief through the years

1

SINCE early morning the rumbling stagecoach had clattered and banged along the rutted, narrow-ribboned trail that seemed to stretch endlessly across the wide, broken West Texas plains, leaving behind a billowing plume of thick dust to mark its passing.

Inside the suspended coach that constantly rocked in every direction in its low-slung leather braces, the four passengers rode in dreary silence, each attempting to avert the threat of motion sickness by concentrated thought. While the uninitiated tended to romanticise the stagecoach, most passengers regarded it as an instrument of sheer torture. Still, it was the fastest means of transportation available, and to professional travellers such as gambler Henry Baines and drummer Gerald

Cogshill, expediency far outweighed the hardships.

Both men were bound for Brackettville, a bustling watering place for the huge wagon trains freighting from San Antonio to California, in hopes of reviving their failing fortunes. The gaunt gambler occupied himself with thoughts of 'knocking down' a big game, while the portly salesman dreamed of fat, bountiful commissions.

Seated across the aisle, the other two passengers tried to ignore the heat and dust that seeped up through the cracks and hung suspended in the late morning sunlight streaming through the windows.

Second Lieutenant Richard Jarrett's mind was on his first post at Fort Clark, outside of Brackettville. He could scarcely believe his good luck. To have 'served at Clark' was nearly equivalent to honourable mention; such an entry in one's record meant that the officer had truly been indoctrinated into army life. He had missed the late War by two years, but a frontier post, with its threat of hostile Indians, Mexican bandits, and other renegades, would offer ample opportunity for glory.

Jarrett absently noticed the two men's eyes again straying to the fashionably dressed young woman beside him, making as close a study of her as they dared without her noticing. He did not blame them; the slender, blue-eyed blonde was far more interesting and pleasing to the eye than the monotonous landscape.

Evelyn Carlisle aloofly ignored the men's glances and pretended to be engrossed in the scenery outside her window. A tall, exquisite beauty, she was accustomed to being admired and had secretly come to expect it. But there was no room for thoughts of vanity, her mind was filled with a mixture of excitement and trepidation at beginning a new life in the wilds of west Texas. It was an unsettling change from the genteel society of New Orleans.

There had been no difference at first; the bayous and moss-hung oak trees of southeast Texas had reminded her of Louisiana. But the change had become more striking the farther west she travelled. Staring out at the pallid, inhospitable wasteland, Evelyn wondered if she possessed the strength and self-reliance necessary to endure the isolation and hardships of a rancher's wife. Then she tried to dismiss her concerns as those of a nervous bride. She loved Travis Dixon and wanted to share his life, wherever that might be.

Evelyn determinedly vowed that she would do everything in her power to make it work. After all, she and hard times were not strangers; the War and its aftermath, the Reconstruction, had introduced them. Her brother had died at Vicksburg; then the loss of their plantation to carpetbaggers had killed her father, and heartbroken, her mother had soon followed him to the grave. But that was all behind her now,

4

destined to become a dim, bittersweet memory. Travis and Texas were to be her life; and he was waiting for her at the next waystation.

She abruptly became aware that the coach had slowed and was moving up a grade. As the angle sharpened she quickly gripped a corner of the window and the seat beneath her, to avoid being spilled down into the aisle or (even more embarrassing) into the laps of the men across from her. The coach shook and trembled as the horses heaved, hoofs digging into the roadbed. Obscuring clouds of chalky dust came boiling inside, now that the stage's headway was slowed.

Finally the coach reached the top and came to a halt on a level stretch. An unaccustomed silence set in, broken occasionally by the wheezing of the lathered team and the creaking of leather thoroughbraces. While the dishevelled passengers resettled themselves in their seats, the driver and guard keenly surveyed the lonely station below.

Except for a string of horses milling in the corral, nothing stirred around the long adobe building or the barn.

The driver fumbled a battered bugle from the boot beneath his seat, spat the grit from his mouth and blew two shrill blasts. Then he and the guard continued their wait.

Presently the front door of the adobe opened. A man wearing a slouch hat and ragged coat of Confederate grey stepped out from the shadowy doorway, waved an arm broadly from side to side, then beckoned the stage down.

"There's old man Hanrahan wavin' us in as usual," the guard drawled, grinning and relaxing his grip on his fifteen-shot Henry repeating rifle.

The grizzled driver grunted and leaned back over the side of the coach. "Barton Wells Station," he bawled to the passengers. "Ten minute stop while we change teams."

With the gruff announcement Evelyn's lovely face lit up and her heartbeat quickened. Instantly her previous

6

weariness was replaced by excited anticipaton at finally being reunited with Travis. A rush of fond memories tumbled through her mind as she visualised his strong, handsome sun-browned face. Then she was jolted from her reveries as the buckskin popper on the driver's blacksnake whip cracked like a rifle shot and set the six horses straining in their trace chains. Evelyn was thrown back against the upholstered seat as the jiggling coach lurched forward and began to roll, gradually picking up speed.

For Evelyn, facing backward, the trip downhill was far easier than the laboured ascent. With her hands now free vanity prevailed. Drawing open the strings of her reticule, she delved inside, withdrew a small, ornate hand mirror and, disregarding the men's mild curiosity, critically inspected her appearance. She almost gasped her distress aloud on seeing her dust-streaked reflection. After three months of separation, she must not greet Travis looking like a lost waif! She snatched out a dainty handkerchief and hurriedly dabbed at her cheeks. It was a futile gesture; dust swirls invaded the coach and taunted her efforts.

"I gather this is where we are to lose the pleasure of your company, Miss Carlisle," Lieutenant Jarrett remarked regretfully, watching her unsuccessful attempts sympathetically, in contrast to the other men's politely repressed amusement.

"Yes, Lieutenant," Evelyn replied, not taking her eyes from the mirror.

"Your fiancé is to be envied," Jarrett said sincerely. His compliment was wasted; Evelyn was too intent on her appearance.

Then the stage also seemed to conspire against Evelyn. Rocking worse than before from its downhill boost in speed as it raced along the flat stretch toward the station, its wheels hit a pothole. She gave an involuntary squeal as her whole side of the coach bucked into the air like a mad bronco and bounced down with a bone-jarring crash. Miraculously, neither the wheels nor axles gave way. The mirror leaped from Evelyn's hand, followed her reticule to the floor, and shattered.

Evelyn stared down at the scattered shards and sadly sighed at her calamity. Not that she was superstitious about seven years' bad luck, but there was now no way to inspect her grooming.

As the stagecoach roared up to the station Hanrahan, who had strangely made no effort to ready fresh horses, began edging back into the shadowy doorway. With one smooth, seemingly unhurried motion, the guard brought the Henry to his shoulder and sent a round squarely through the man's chest.

Dead on his feet, the disguised Comanche tottered and collapsed, his moccasined feet kicking up in the doorway.

Before the guard could eject the spent shell from the Henry's chamber, a ragged fusillade erupted and rosy flames blossomed from the adobe's doorway and windows. Screaming and jerking in unison, he and the driver sprawled limply into the front boot and the terrified team was left to run wild. Painted, half-naked Comanches spilled from the building and ran in howling pursuit.

More bloodcurdling war whoops filled the air as a large band of swarthy horsemen whipped their thin, wiry ponies around the far corner of the long adobe and cut off the runaway stage. Then, some circling, others fidgeting back and forth in a confused trampling of many unshod hoofs, the shrieking Comanches descended on the coach.

So swiftly had it all happened that only now did the startled passengers realise their danger and react. What followed lasted only a few minutes, but each second seemed to stretch into an eternity of brutal action.

Her grooming forgotten Evelyn, frozen in heart-stopping fright, sat staring out in trancelike fascination at the clamouring, disorderly mass of gaudy paint, flashing steel, and fluttering feathers surging about her through the thick clouds of dust as someone inside yelled, "Comanches!"

The will to act was also frozen in Gerald Cogshill. Clutching a pepperbox derringer, the drummer sat wide-eyed and slack-jawed, oblivious to the quivering arrow that drove into the window frame. He remained paralysed, even when a bronzed, muscular arm thrust a scalp-decorated lance through the window and into his chest, pinning him against the seat like a fat bug.

Cogshill gave a gurgling cry and gaped stupidly at the long shaft affixed with tufts of bright hair that had suddenly taken root and became a part of him. Mouth opening and closing, he half turned his head to announce this wonder to his fellow passengers, but no one seemed interested. His fast-glazing eyes returned to the scalp-ornamented lance and a wry grin crossed his face an instant before the life left his body with a mighty shudder that toppled his beaver hat from his bald head.

While Lieutenant Jarrett frantically pawed at the holster flap imprisoning his service revolver, gambler Henry Baines drew a .36 Navy Colt from his shoulder holster with blurring speed and blasted a hideously painted face at the window to bloody ruin. The gunshot boomed deafeningly inside the violently rocking coach and added its white powder smoke to the choking, dust-tainted air. Baines' second shot crashed through a round buffalo-hide shield rimmed with smoked and hooped scalps and slammed a mounted brave to the ground, where a multitude of stamping hoofs quickly turned him into unrecognisable pulp. Heedless of the arrows and bullets flying about him, Baines grimly continued pumping shells into the close swirl of brown bodies.

Jarrett succeeded in freeing his pistol and turned to Evelyn, who sat rigid and white-faced, the back of her hand pressed to her mouth. Her large eyes were locked on Cogshill's glassy eyes, as though they were engaged in a ghastly staring contest. Jarrett grabbed her wrist and hurled her down into the aisle an instant before an arrow sank into her seat. Then he sent a .44 slug into the vermilion-streaked forehead of a Comanche who was attempting to slither through the coach window and hurtled him backwards into the throng behind him.

Small, stylish hat askew, Evelyn raised her head from the floor, only to recoil with a frightened gasp as an arrowhead punched through the door panel and halted before her face, its sharp metal tip quivering with spent force. Her lips moved soundlessly, a scream worming its way up from deep inside her constricted chest as the shock of near death shattered her dreamlike state, awakening her to horrid reality.

Rolling onto her side and thrusting herself up onto an elbow, Evelyn brushed the hat from her head and squinted through the blinding dust and acrid gunsmoke at the violence playing out around her. The two men's six-guns roared like cannons inside the close confines of the coach, while outside the Comanches' piercing, hawklike screams — so peculiar that once heard they were never forgotten — were punctuated by the firing of their own weapons. She was trapped in a nightmare of sight and sound.

And there was no escape.

Black broadcloth frock coat streaked red, Baines cursed mindlessly and squeezed off another round into the rushing pack. A Comanche catapulted backwards, a large hole in the left side of his chest. Baines gasped in anguish as a slug tore a deep, ragged groove under his right cheekbone. The searing pain brought a moment's distraction, and a Comanche reached the coach door and yanked it open. Baines' revolver clicked on an empty chamber.

As the yelping, painted and feathered brave started to climb inside Baines quickly reversed his Colt and turned it into a club. A savage blow from the pistol butt cracked the Indian's greasy black head open and he dropped like a pole-axed steer. Other braves loomed outside the door. Baines discarded his Colt and instantly twin .41 derringers leaped out from their sleeve holsters and into his hands. With two deadly blasts he momentarily cleared the doorway.

Breath rasping nervously between bared teeth, Jarrett squinted beneath the low bill of his forage cap at the savage throng manoeuvring still closer. His eyes were drawn to a tall, gold adorned warrior, lance raised high above his spreading war bonnet of splendid eagle plumes, whom he took to be their chief.

Bring him down, and the Comanches would withdraw!

Jarrett coolly sighted on the chiefs brown, muscular chest and slowly squeezed the trigger. The heavy Colt bucked in his hand and a cloud of white smoke blotted out all before him.

At that exact moment a yipping brave unwittingly galloped between them and was blasted from his horse's bare back. Arms and legs jerking grotesquely, he was dead before he hit the ground.

The smoke cleared and Jarrett was stunned and disheartened to see the war chief still astride his decorated pony. How could he have missed? Before he could find an answer something walloped his chest and jolted him back against the seat. There was no pain, but he felt strangely numb, right down to his boots. He grunted and jerked again as something else struck him, this time in the stomach, and the numbness climbed higher.

Jarrett lowered his eyes and saw blood staining and spreading over the front of his buttoned tunic. His first impulse was to try and brush the tunic clean, but the effort seemed too great. Besides, he would be no more successful than Miss Carlisle had been with her attempted grooming. That thought brought his eyes down to where she lay, tangled golden hair framing her pale face, terrified blue eyes enormous above high delicate cheekbones.

She would certainly be a prize for the Comanches.

Jarrett grimly knew what he must do. It would be an act of charity. Pitting his last ounce of concentrated will against death itself, he raised the Colt before his almost sightless eyes, took aim at the confused woman and pulled the trigger.

The round misfired.

But Jarrett never knew. His lifeless body pitched forward and landed heavily on top of Evelyn Carlisle, pinning her to the floor in a ghastly lovers' embrace. Screaming hysterically, she struggled vainly to dislodge his bloodstained corpse.

On the other side of the coach Henry Baines dropped two warriors with his last two shots. His hand started for the sheathed bowie knife on his hip, but the movement was never completed. An arrow drove through his chest and his convulsing body toppled through the doorway, where a waiting pack immediately descended upon it with a frenzy of knives and lances.

Evelyn Carlisle was too absorbed in wrestling with the dead lieutenant's imprisoning body to notice that the gunshots had stopped. She heard only her own wailing, erratic gasps and her heartbeat throbbing wildly in her ears. The coach door suddenly banged open and she squeezed her eyes shut against the sun's stabbing glare. A rough hand touched her cheek and she opened her blinking eyes to a vision of utter horror.

Looming above her was an inverted, swarthy face ugly and vicious in every detail. Beneath coarse black hair, plaited in two braids and crowned with two feathers, the paint-smeared forehead was low, the similarly smeared cheekbones extremely wide. A long knife scar ran down one smallpox pitted cheek and turned up the corner of his mouth in a harsh, leering grin.

With an exuberant cry he seized her shoulders and began tugging her out from under the dead man.

Evelyn screamed, struggling in complete terror, and resisted his efforts by now trying to shelter herself under Jarrett's limp form like a turtle withdrawing inside its shell. Both arms of her dress ripped free at the shoulders as she was dragged forward inch by protesting inch. Intent on raking out his small, fierce eyes, her long nails frantically sought his elusive face. Then her head and shoulders were hauled through the doorway. One of his hands cruelly twisted her hair, raising her drooped head, while the other drew a large wicked-looking knife. A single sob escaped Evelyn's throat as she realised his intent and froze, staring up in nameless anguish at the glinting blade poised to strike.

She was going to be scalped alive.

2

THE knife plunged downward in a deadly arc.

Suddenly a feathered lance thrust forward and, steel rasping against steel, halted the blade midway above Evelyn. A voice barked a sharp guttural command. Reluctantly the savage released Evelyn and stepped away, sheathing his knife. The lance withdrew and the voice snapped another command.

Quickly three braves vaulted from their scrawny-maned ponies and went to Evelyn. They jerked her from the coach and set her on her unsteady feet before a tall, bronze warrior astride a black stallion, its mane and tail decorated with bright feathers. Hollow and numb, Evelyn hesitantly studied her apparent benefactor.

A magnificent bonnet of eagle feathers

framed his broad, painted, strong-boned face, with its dark, sunken eyes, prominent hooked nose and thin, hard mouth. A large crudely-fashioned gold necklace on his bare, muscular chest glittered blinding in the sunlight.

Evelyn tried to raise a hand to shield her eyes from the reflection, but the brave tightened his restraining grip on her bare arm. She gasped and tensed against her captors as the feathered lance dipped, poked curiously at her billowing skirt, then lifted its hem to reveal her petticoats and stockinged ankles. Trembling slightly, she ignored the probing lance and kept her large eyes fastened on the tall warrior's impassive face. The lance slowly retreated and she drew a shaky breath. The chief spoke imperiously and before she could move one brave wrenched her arms behind her back and held them while the other two braves leaned down and grabbed her skirt.

"No . . . please . . . stop!" Evelyn cried in distress as the material parted in a series of mournful screeches. Her words went unheeded. Under their clawing, tearing hands her petticoats came away and her stockings were peeled down her long legs. Cheeks burning, tears of indignation welling in her wide eyes, Evelyn writhed helplessly in the brave's firm grasp as a circle of onlookers hooted and laughed derisively. She kicked at a tormentor's face with a high heel. He effortlessly caught her slim ankle, wrenched off her shoe and then her stocking. At last the ordeal was over and her skirt, torn high on one side, hung in jagged tatters about her knees.

The chief's appraising gaze travelled the length of her slender form, lingering for a moment on the swell of her bosom above the tight bodice, then moving down to her lovely ivory legs. He uttered another imperious order and the three braves started to haul Evelyn away.

With a protesting cry the scar-faced brave stalked forward gesturing toward

Evelyn and spoke hotly to his chief. Evelyn did not need to know Comanche to gather the sinister importance of their strangely high-pitched, guttural, sing-song words. She grimly wondered if a quick death at the scar-faced brave's hands would be preferable to what his chief had planned for her. Before she could dwell on that morbid dilemma the men's heated argument came to an abrupt end as the chief's moccasined foot caught the brave full in the face and slammed him to the ground in a shower of dust.

Shaking his head dazedly, the brave sat up trembling in rage and his hand went to his sheathed knife. The feathered lance shot forward, its sharp point gouging blood from the buck's bare chest, and slowly forced him down flat on his back. For a tense moment poisoned stares passed between the two. Then, very slowly, the defiance drained from the brave's blood smeared face and he wisely yielded.

The chief spoke harshly, backing

up his words by gashing more blood from the unflinching brave's chest, then raised the lance and motioned impatiently to the Indians holding Evelyn. One buck released her and hurried ahead while the others dragged her away. The chief paid no heed as the scar-faced brave climbed to his feet and, wiping the blood from his face, stood glaring after them.

Evelyn was hastily propelled through the parting circle of hostile, painted faces to where the third buck was waiting with a decorated pony. Her wrists were lashed together behind her; other lengths of rawhide secured her arms against her body. She was hoisted across the blanket and rawhide saddle, roughly forced to sit upright, and fastened in place by a thong connecting her ankles under the horse's belly. Their task completed, two braves left to join the looters while the third remained, holding the pony's horsehair lead rope. No other braves came near so Evelyn was allowed to study the

Comanches in relative safety.

Naked but for breechclout and moccasins, most were short and thickset, with very bowed legs that caused them to waddle somewhat as they walked. Their heads seemed almost too large for their bodies; small, deepset eyes stared out from broad, flat, hairless faces streaked with crude-coloured paint. All wore one or more feathers in their dark braided hair, and an occasional necklace of bone or silver.

Evelyn shivered despite the warm wind that caressed her bare arms and legs. It was as if she were watching the Mongols or some other ancient barbaric tribe. But at the moment there appeared no threat. The Comanches were having a wonderful time, prancing and cavorting like children, as they flourished various articles of clothing from the strewn luggage. Tears came to her eyes as she sadly watched her beautiful dresses ripped apart by a multitude of eager hands. A buck capered about in her torn petticoats;

two others were engaged in a tug of war with one of her stockings.

Then the light-hearted scene turned ugly.

Lieutenant Jarrett's body was dumped from the stage and stripped of its bloody tunic. A warrior grabbed a hank of the dead man's hair and leaned over with a large knife.

Evelyn gasped in stunned horror and tried to cover her eyes. She couldn't. Her hands were tightly tied. She wrenched at the confining rawhide thongs. Her struggles were useless. She knew she should turn away, but a perverse fascination compelled her to watch while the warrior made a deft circular incision in a small part of the corpse's scalp.

That was strange. She had always thought scalping took the whole top of the head off.

Every muscle taut, Evelyn stared in wide-eyed revulsion as the warrior gave a quick, powerful jerk. With a sound like tearing muslin, the scalplock came free. Howling gleefully, the warrior leaped up and danced about brandishing his trophy. Several braves whooped and danced with him.

Ashen, Evelyn swayed in the saddle and fought back the bile that tried to rise into her throat. Carefully averting her eyes from Jarrett's mutilated body, she concentrated on breathing slowly and deeply until her overwrought senses cleared. Then she was startled by Comanche war whoops and craned her neck towards the far end of the adobe, where several bucks were driving the horses from the corral. They were joined by others herding the unhitched stage horses and the ponies of dead warriors. The groups merged in a swirl, and with a thunder of hoofs and farewell shrieks, galloped off in a rolling dust cloud.

Evelyn became conscious of eyes upon her before she even heard the soft thud of unshod hoofs. She turned and instantly went rigid as the Comanche chief drew in his pony beside her. His stern gaze raked her from head to bare toes and she knew he was not merely inspecting her snug bonds. She tried to meet his eyes boldly; her cool, haughty, ladylike demeanour had well intimidated many a New Orleans dandy. Unfortunately, the painted savage before her was no New Orleans dandy.

Her bravado was short-lived. Her lips drew back with an involuntary gasp as he reached out, and almost gently, brushed a wave of dishevelled hair back from her face. He fingered a lock, his eyes comparing its colour to the gold of his necklace, and a hint of a smile slowly twisted the corners of his mouth. Evelyn suddenly wondered if he had claimed her golden scalp for himself. Then logic told her that she would not still be alive. She was either to be his hostage or his squaw. Neither prospect was appealing — but then neither was death.

The chief leaned down and took her pony's lead rope from the brave, who strode away. He glanced about at the scavenging band and barked a guttural order that sent them scrambling to their ponies. Then he nudged his horse forward and started off at a brisk trot. As the others fell in behind, Evelyn noticed the scar-faced brave among them. His malicious eyes and horrid, disfigured smile plainly said he was only awaiting the right opportunity to take her scalp. Evelyn repressed a shudder and looked away in time to catch a last glimpse of her ruined possessions scattered about the rear boot of the stagecoach. Everything she owned in the world was lost, reduced to memories.

For the first time since her capture Evelyn found that she was capable of another emotion besides fear; hatred. That emotion swept away all self-pity and brought a new strength. She had endured damnyankees and carpetbaggers, and now she would endure Comanches. No matter the hardships she was determined to survive and see them in their graves. Travis would find her and see to that. This forced separation from him further strengthened her hatred and resolve.

Lance tossed high, the chief let out a chilling victory yell and kicked his horse into a gallop. The others joined in. Shrill cries hanging in the still air, the Comanches and their captive rode from the massacre site and were swallowed up by their pursuing dust.

★ ★ ★

Travis Dixon was a happy man. But that did not blind him to the possible dangers on the trail. As he guided the jouncing buckboard along his sharp eyes were in constant motion, scanning the uneven expanse before him. Except for the four years of war, he had spent the rest of his thirty-three years on the raw west Texas frontier, and such vigilance had become second nature.

Last night had been a 'Comanche Moon', full, white, and almost as bright as day, and with it invariably came the red raiders and their scavengers, the Kiowas. The Comanches were bad enough, but the Kiowas were even worse. Torture was their single art, and they delighted and excelled at it. As a precaution he had camped dry last night, and so far he hadn't come across any Indian signs. But that didn't mean they weren't out there somewhere lying in wait.

Reassured by the feel of the bowie knife and Colt .44 on either hip and the sixteen-shot Winchester '66 leaning against his right leg, Travis let his thoughts again return to Evelyn Carlisle, his beautiful, soon-to-be bride. A squint up at the sun told him it was a good hour or so past noon. Evelyn might already be waiting at the waystation, if the stage kept to its schedule — which was highly unlikely. With the Comanche threat he was beginning to doubt his decision not to meet Evelyn in Brackettville, but that would have added an extra day both ways to the two-day trip to his ranch.

Travis' lean, weather-creased face twisted up in a thoughtful scowl as he adjusted the wide brim of his black, flat-crowned hat. It had been his idea to be married at the ranch. The circuit preacher and his nearest neighbours were set to be there Saturday afternoon. Barring unforseen delays, he and Evelyn should arrive home midday Friday, giving her time to rest up beforehand.

Friends had ragged him about throwing his loop over a fancy New Orleans filly instead of some downhome mustang. He had to admit it was going to be a whopping big change for Evelyn, but he was sure she had the grit to stick it out. Though ranching was hard there was now a chance to make it pay off in a big way, despite the oppressive Reconstruction that was imposed on the South.

The Long Drive of '66 to Sedalia, Missouri had ended in despair, with herds stopped at Baxter Springs, Kansas because of marauding Jayhawkers, and irate farmers complaining about the Texas fever ticks carried by longhorns. But now Joe McCoy, an Illinois cattle-buyer, had built vast stockpens at a place called Abilene, in north-central Kansas, away from the sodbusters and outlaw gangs. With a four dollar steer selling for forty dollars back East, he and Evelyn would do right well. Given five years, he would turn the ranch into the showplace that her plantation had been before the War.

Travis' mind was still on his big plans for the future when he topped a small rise and halted to let the weary team blow. It was then he noticed the buzzards circling high in the cloudless, heat-blurred sky right in the area where the Barton Wells Station stood. Squinting through the shimmering heat vapours, he could just make out the distant buildings. He tried to tell himself that maybe one of the relay horses had died, but too many buzzards were gathered for just a horse. Only a fool could mistake their ominous meaning.

Travis sat fretting, icy fear-sweat worming down his broad back beneath his checkered flannel shirt at the involuntary thought of Evelyn lying dead in her own blood, a scalplock torn from her blonde head: He ran a splayed hand over his grimy face and chased the terrible image from his mind, then picked up the Winchester. Grimly jacking a shell into its chamber, he lay the rifle across his knees and urged the team into a trot.

★ ★ ★

The swaying back door flew open under Travis' boot heel and crashed back against the wall. In a half crouch he burst inside, rifle sweeping the large room.

The place stank of Comanches. Old Hanrahan's mutilated body, stripped to soiled long johns, was sprawled in a twisted, unnatural position amid the wreckage of the make-shift board and barrel bar. The dried contents of several busted bottles had mixed their colours with his blood and moccasins had spread the stains all over the rough, splintered floor. Tables and chairs were overturned; the coffee pot added its stains around the stove, but the large pot of stew had been devoured.

Drawing his lanky frame to its full height, Travis crossed to the narrow hallway and followed it, cautiously checking the few rooms on either side. They were empty, except one. Jess Kobeck, Hanrahan's helper, lay peacefully on his bloodstained bunk, evidently murdered in his sleep. Travis walked back down the ball, stepped over the dead Comanche in the doorway wearing Hanrahan's clothes, and, bracing himself for what he might find, strode toward the bodies strewn round the unhitched stagecoach.

A dozen Comanches frozen in awkward postures of sudden, violent death testified to the fierce fight the occupants of the stage had waged before their slaughter. Thick black swarms of annoyed, humming flies begrudgingly rose from the corpses at Travis' approach, their beating wings spreading the cloying stench of death over the still air. Sparing a cursory glance at the mutilated, partly stripped driver and young soldier, Travis hesitantly went to the stage door and looked inside. To his relief there was only a bald-headed drummer with a gaping hole in his chest drawing flies. The frozen grin on his fat face seemed to say he didn't mind.

At the stage's rear boot Travis found a woman's ruined possessions scattered in with the men's things. Desperately hoping it had been another woman, he sifted through the smashed trunk and came upon a packet of letters tied in a blue ribbon. There was no mistaking the handwriting on the envelopes.

It was his own.

Clutching the packet, he knelt there

as helpless anger and frustration clamped around him, squeezing the breath from his chest. His teeth ached from the savageness with which he had clenched them together. He was so concentrated on his tragedy that his sharp ears did not detect the faint movement behind him until it was almost too late.

Travis turned and saw a Comanche, one side of his painted face covered with dry blood from a scalp wound, coming at him with a raised tomahawk. The packet fell to the ground as his hand shot up and caught the Indian's thick wrist, halting the glinting tomahawk scarcely a hairs-breadth from his face. The strong momentum carried Travis backward and he brought his legs up, caught the brave in the stomach and flipped him high over his head. The warrior smashed to the ground in a cloud of dust, but bounded to his feet and came at him again. Travis gained his feet, his hand flashing to his holster.

It was empty. The Colt had fallen

free when he had tossed the Comanche.

Travis leaped back, avoiding a low, murderous belly slash. His left hand went to his sheath, found the bowie knife still there. Yanking it out, he flipped the blade to his right hand and dropped into a crouch.

The men circled warily, weapons meeting metallically as they feinted, advancing and retreating, testing each other's reflexes. Nimbly avoiding the strewn luggage they stormed about in strained silence. Flies buzzed their sweaty faces, threatening distraction; a careless movement of eye or hand meant death from a vicious swipe by knife or tomahawk.

With sudden speed they slammed together with a savage impact and wrestled chest to chest in a desperate fury. The Indian jerked a knee up at Travis' groin. He twisted aside, took the blow on his outer thigh, then spat in his foe's eyes. Loosening his grip on Travis' wrist, the Comanche staggered back momentarily blinded by spittle.

Travis released the man's wrist and smashed a fist into his painted face. The Comanche stumbled backward, tangled a foot in a torn dress and sprawled to the ground. Before he could rise Travis was on him like a cougar.

Ruined clothing attempting to cling to their thrashing bodies, they rolled over and over in the stifling dust and came to a halt against a rear wheel. Travis pinned the man and banged his tomahawk hand against the wheel again and again. Slowly the bruised and bloodied fingers reluctantly uncurled from the handle. As the tomahawk fell, Travis switched his grip to the brave's throat and burrowed his fingers deeply into his windpipe.

Face turning purple beneath his war paint, the Comanche writhed and surged violently beneath Travis, who clung tenaciously and forced his knife downward, inch by protested inch. Then the blade seemed locked in place, hovering above the buck's heaving chest. Beads of sweat stood out on Travis' forehead, cut grooves down his taut, dusty face and stung his eyes with salt before dropping onto the Indian's grimacing face. Travis abruptly bent at the waist and sank down heavily on his knife hand, letting his body weight drive the blade the contested distance into the brave's chest. It sank to the hilt and he gave a vicious twist. The brave spasmed madly, fighting against death, then life left his body in a prolonged half cry, half rasping sigh.

Travis wrenched the knife free, stumbled to his feet, and the flies quickly took his place atop the corpse. He wiped his knife clean on the soiled remnants of a man's white ruffled shirt, then collected his hat and guns and went to fetch the team and buckboard from behind a cluster of rocks outside the station grounds.

Returning with the buckboard, Travis took saddles from the barn, unhitched and saddled the team, and packed the saddlebags with supplies. The tracks showed the band had split; as the group herding horses would not want to be burdened with a captive, Travis elected to follow the larger party. Pausing to retrieve his packet of letters, he started off with both horses. The Comanches had a good head start, but by borrowing one of their own tricks and switching back and forth on the horses, he should be able to cut that lead respectably.

His lean face a mask of ruthless determination, Travis nudged his horse into a gallop and followed the Comanches' trail toward the bleak, distant mountains looming in the southwest.

3

FOR Evelyn Carlisle the arduous journey was a silent nightmare from which she could not awaken no matter how hard she tried. Her savage captors barely spoke, and their horses' hoofs were muffled by the chalky white sand that extended in every direction, so featureless that nothing seemed to mark their progress. The distant mountains appeared no closer than they had hours ago. It was as if they were riding in place, snared between burning earth and sky, cruelly fated to spend eternity in an earthly hell.

Evelyn was already enduring the torments of hell. Suffering etched her exquisite face. Every nerve and muscle in her tall, slender body cried its anguish. Reeling with exhaustion, she clung in the saddle only through utter will and self-preservation. With her wrists and arms rigidly lashed behind her and her ankles connected beneath the pony, a fatal slip would hurl her down under the galloping, unshod hoofs. Dispelling the horrid image, she determinedly forced her complaining long legs to retain their grip on the horse's sides.

The sun was lower, but Evelyn had no accurate idea how long they'd held this relentless pace. Only once had they paused briefly to let the horses blow, and during that time she had remained mounted, without a chance to properly ease her cramped muscles. The memory made Evelyn once more damn her unfeeling captors, for about the hundredth time since they had intruded into her life. Then she told herself she should be grateful for their indifference — especially, the scar-faced brave who still gave her hostile glances as they rode.

Evelyn had heard contradictory stories about the fate of white women taken captive by the Indians. Safe in civilised New Orleans, she had always dismissed most as tales calculated to horrify or titillate the fantasies of schoolgirls and old maids. Fantasy was one thing, reality quite another. Right now she would gladly trade places with any pubescent schoolgirl. She remembered Travis and others with frontier experience were taciturn on the subject around women. Lieutenant Jarrett's earnest attempt to shoot her before dying was all the proof she needed. Still, she refused to despair. Two men had tried to kill her today, each for a different reason, and had failed. She was meant to live — and not as an illiterate savage's white squaw. God could not be that cruel. Travis *was* coming for her. She must never stop believing that. The slender thread of hope was all that stitched together her fragile self-control after the horrors she had witnessed this day.

Her courage bolstered, Evelyn ignored

the painted band closely pressed in around her and kept her eyes locked on their chief's broad, bronzed shoulders and madly fluttering war bonnet while they rode on in eerie silence.

* * *

Racing hoofs chewing up the miles across the vast expanse, Travis Dixon continued his ruthless pursuit and tried not to give in to the thoughts that bedevilled him. He *would* find Evelyn alive and rescue her — and in doing so his vengeance would extract a heavy toll on her captors. Their trail led in the general direction of Brackettville and Fort Clark, but he knew the Comanches would change course before long and probably head south after the group with the horses.

Travis considered, then dismissed the idea of seeking help. Brackettville was too full of scalawags who'd as soon rob and kill somebody on the trail than go fight Indians. The Yankee cavalry was still pretty raw, only having re-garrisoned Fort Clark in mid-December of last year. Besides, they would be useless if the Comanches crossed the Rio Grande. Only the Rangers wouldn't hesitate entering Mexico, but the Reconstruction had forced their disbandment. Their successors, the State Police, were lackeys of the carpetbaggers and preferred enforcing their tyranny rather than fighting Indians; foreclosures were safer — and more profitable.

The wheezing, frothing bay was starting to stumble with fatigue; it was now time to switch back to the sorrel. Slowing the pace, Travis drew the other horse alongside, kicked his feet free from the stirrups, leaned out and, grasping the pommel, smoothly made the transfer. He planted himself firmly in the saddle, continued for a bit at the slower run, letting the bay drop behind and catch its wind some, then booted the sorrel into full gallop. He knew before long he would be forced to halt and let both horses blow; dead horses wouldn't do him, or Evelyn, any good. But until that time Travis was determined to keep whittling down the miles that separated them.

* * *

The late afternoon sun scorched its way across the brassy sky, and its slow descent offered no let up from its oppressive heat.

Evelyn could not endure another minute of agony atop the galloping pony. Mind and body thoroughly exhausted, she felt her knees slowly loosening their grip on the horse's lathered, mud-caked sides. Her pain-drugged mind no longer cared; death would be a blessing. Just as she felt herself start to slip sideways her horse was yanked to a quick halt.

For the first time in hours the Comanches broke their silence, laughing and making what seemed to be good-natured comments, as a multitude of shrill, high-pitched barks were heard ahead. Curiously peering through a golden spider web of windblown hair partly masking her face, Evelyn saw a prairie dog village stretching for more than a quarter of a mile cross the flat area before her. Alerted by the ponies' hoofs, hundreds of the fat, dun-coloured little creatures were swishing their short tails and diving into the safety of their small, volcano-like mounds that dotted the entire area. Evelyn momentarily forgot her weariness and stared in fascination at the scurrying, squirrel-like rodents. Then she felt hands on her bare ankles and tensely looked down to see two braves untying them.

The warrior who had previously been appointed her protector reached up and pulled Evelyn from the pony by her waist and forearm. Numb from long hours of riding her legs refused to support her and she fell heavily against the man's painted chest, almost carrying him to the ground. Her nostrils were immediately assailed by sweat, foul breath and buffalo grease. Stumbling, the short man righted himself and, arms circling her waist, half dragged, half carried her toward a thin strip of shade before a cluster of rocks while her bare toes dug furrows across the warm sand. He dumped her with her back against a gritty rock and walked away without bothering to bind her ankles.

Once again Evelyn's captors were indifferent, milling about tending their ponies and talking in low, guttural tones. Resting her head back against the rock, Evelyn chanced closing her wary eyes and let herself go limp for a long moment, wincing and worrying her softly moulded lower lip between even white teeth as fiery pinpricks danced up and down the length of her legs with the sluggish return of her circulation. Then her watchdog came up with a canteen. The markings on its side identified it as an army canteen, probably taken from a dead trooper.

He kneeled and raised the canteen to her dry lips. Evelyn gulped the lukewarm water gratefully and tried not to cough as it overflowed her mouth and trickled down her chin. All too soon the canteen was withdrawn. She eyed him imploringly, but the brave shook his head, spoke in his native tongue and rubbed his bare belly. Evelyn gathered he was saying that too much water suddenly would make her sick.

The high-pitched, sing-song chatter abruptly ceased as the Comanches directed their attention to a whirl of dust on top of a small bluff on one side of the prairie dog village. The dust cleared to reveal a pack of mounted warriors silhouetted against the dying sun. Armed mostly with lances and bows, they sat their scrawny ponies and stared down intently.

Evelyn sensed the tension and divided her glances between the Comanches and the newcomers. Even though she was unfamiliar with Indians she could tell the watchers were different. Their attitude was even more savage and predatory, like a pack of skulking jackals. Bare legs dangling stirrupless, they sat bent over their ponies' necks and cast hungry eyes down at her and the Comanches' plunder. Her guard confirmed her suspicion.

"Kiowa," he muttered, more to himself than to her, and spat contemptuously.

The Comanche chieftain barked a terse command and the others made an elaborate display of nonchalance as they slowly began preparing to leave. This time Evelyn's guard was almost gentle as he drew her up on her still unsteady feet and, gripping an arm, unhurriedly led her toward her pony, almost as if escorting her onto a cotillion dance floor. Evelyn was boosted astride her pony and her ankles again joined together by rawhide. The brave swung atop his pony and took her horse's lead rope. The chief was too preoccupied acting the mighty warrior for the Kiowas' benefit to bother with a mere squaw. With a wave of his lance he regally led the way out into the flat area.

Letting their horses pick the way, the Comanches skirted the far side of the prairie dog town, keeping it between them and the watching Kiowas. Evelyn was the only one to look directly toward the bluff, until a brave rode alongide and growled a menacing order that she rightly took to mean not to do so. She obeyed and stared at her guard's back. The man who had spoken gave a satisfied grunt and allowed his pony to again fall behind.

Frontier stories came unbidden into Evelyn's mind. She remembered hearing that, surprisingly, the fiercest battles waged by Indians were among themselves. Their inability to unite would eventually spell their downfall. She was aware of the hostility between the two tribes, and had no wish to be helplessly caught in the middle of a battle. While her present captors were frightening, the Kiowas were truly terrifying. She felt a change of hands would mean even greater suffering, and finally end in certain death.

Silently fuming and sulking the Kiowas sat gazing like famine wolves at the unattainable band below. A headlong charge would result in the loss of their ponies before they were even halfway across the wide, miniature crater-pitted prairie dog village. Reluctantly accepting defeat they turned and slunk from the skyline.

The slight relaxation of their rigid postures was the Comanches' only acknowledgement of the Kiowas' departure. Evelyn sensed the lessening of tension and braved a backward glance up at the empty bluff. She received no reprimand, but the scar-faced brave's malevolent eyes caught hers and made her turn back.

One danger had passed, but Evelyn grimly knew that she would not be safe as long as she was a Comanche captive.

The Comanche Moon made the trail easy enough to follow, and splashed Travis Dixon's lean frame in its brilliant light that reflected off the surrounding white sands. Jawline tight, Travis heard only the creak of saddle leather over the horses' pounding hoofbeats. He was a man obsessed, his mind filled with thoughts of bloody revenge. Since he still had not come across Evelyn's mutilated body it was safe to assume she was going to be kept alive, either as a squaw or object of trade. Then again, Indians were irrational and you could never be entirely sure of just what they would do.

Travis tried not to recall the times he had ridden with Rangers and neighbours in pursuit of raiding parties, only to tragically find their captives had died unspeakable deaths of insane, prolonged anguish. Even with women Indians respected how they died, and certain fiendish refinements of degradation and torment were practised, depending upon the time allowed and the victim's endurance. Travis' face grew even harder beneath its pale, dusty mask and his mouth set in the tight cruel line of a killer. His mind was so full of hate that he paid little attention to the cloud bank drifting over the moon as he galloped along at break-neck speed. It was as though his own dark thoughts had closed in about him, shutting out all light and shrouding him with their malevolence.

It happened suddenly, without warning.

There was a loud, sickening snap of bone. The bay screamed hideously and abruptly went down, hurling Travis somersaulting through black space. He heard the sorrel add its terrified screams to those of the bay, and then the ground rose up to meet him. Travis somehow managed to land loose-limbed, but that did not keep the wind from leaving his lungs in a sharp rush. Fighting nausea and dizziness, he rolled with the fall and was dimly aware that he was tumbling over small mounds, crushing them beneath his weight. Then before he realised it, he was lying motionless and dazedly staring up at a pair of huge, pallid moons through a red haze streaked with shooting stars.

For a time sky and earth whirled in a giddying blur, then the moons slowly merged into one. Travis lay feeling the heat of the day still retained in the sand beneath him while he summoned the needed strength to sit up. Every bone and muscle complaining, his body begrudgingly obeyed. He ached like blazes, but nothing was broken. He stood and, swaying ungainly, surveyed his surroundings.

Small mounds, many a foot or so high, sprawled haphazardly as far as he could see. He had blundered right into a prairie dog town.

The bay's piteous cries halted the curse he was about to utter and Travis turned to see the downed animal, right foreleg flapping awkwardly below the knee, unsuccessfully trying to stand. The sorrel was nowhere to be seen.

He was alone in the desert with a crippled horse.

4

GIRDING himself for what he must do, Travis picked up his hat, moved to his fallen pistol, and shook off the dust before returning it to its holster. He went to the thrashing bay and spoke soothingly while he stripped off the canteen, bedroll and saddlebags. The whinnying, pain-crazed horse showered froth with every toss of its head as it continued heaving and kicking to regain its feet. Leaving the saddle in place, Travis stood and reached for his Colt. He abruptly hesitated, hand frozen on the gun butt.

A shot would carry for miles across the still desert, alerting anyone within its range. It would be an open invitation to any curious Kiowa or Comanche.

Travis stared down at the tormented bay. Compassion told him he could not go off and leave the animal in misery. The pistol was out, but there was another way.

Kneeling, he caught the bridle and forced the horse down flat on its side. He stroked and spoke softly as he stretched its long neck out on the pale sand. The bay settled down somewhat under his gentle ministrations, its breath coming in sobbing snorts. The moonlight and tautness of the bay's oustretched neck aided Travis in locating its large throat artery. He would have preferred a swift clean kill but there was no choice. He reluctantly eased the bowie knife from its sheath and deftly severed the artery. Wheezing and coughing, the horse wallowed for a long moment, then was mercifully still. Travis wiped the knife on the animal's flank and sheathed it once more.

After gathering his gear Travis grimly took stock of his situation. The sorrel was gone, taking with it the extra water and supplies, and most of all, the Winchester. It would be a waste of time trying to backtrack and find the horse. Time was something neither he nor Evelyn had. With any luck the Comanches were camped for the night, giving him a chance to narrow the gap separating them. But he sure couldn't do much on foot, and any small gain would be quickly lost as soon as the Comanches broke camp at sunrise.

Well, there was no sense fretting. Right now he had to concern himself with covering as much ground as he could in the cool of night. Come dawn the desert would start warming up, and by noon he'd better have found a place to hunker down in until the heat of day had past.

The broad Comanche Moon lighting the way, Travis Dixon solemnly began following the tracks of unshod ponies that weaved through the seemingly endless prairie dog village. Once away from the tangled snares he set off, running fifty steps and then walking fifty. The encumbering bedroll, canteen and saddlebags weighed heavily on him, but Travis was determined to hold to the brisk pace as long as possible.

Each step was taking him closer to Evelyn.

★ ★ ★

Wrists tied before her, long legs attached at her crossed ankles, Evelyn sat on one of the smelly horse blankets that had previously served as her saddle. The other equally vile blanket was draped about her shoulders. It was shivering cold in the mountain clearing, and odorous or not, she wasn't about to forsake the scant warmth. Though utterly exhausted and numbed by weariness, she also was not about to forsake her meagre meal of cured venison strips and water, from the army canteen. Awkward with her bound hands, she ate and drank slowly while attempting to close her delicate nostrils to the stench. She bit off another piece of the tough, stringy strip she held and watched her captors as she chewed.

Her guard and the others sat talking in guttural tones around a small fire of dry branches that emitted a hot flame and were almost smokeless. Evelyn envied their warmth. Then she apprehensively cowered within herself as their chief rose and stoically approached. The braves seemed to take no notice of his departure. She chewed hurriedly and swallowed as he reached her. For a long moment neither spoke. Clutching the remaining strip of meat, Evelyn mutely gazed up at his flint-hard face while his cold, black eyes slowly regarded her.

"I am Stone Eagle, war chief of the Comanches," he solemnly announced.

"Y . . . you speak English . . ." Evelyn stammered, shocked.

"Learn much from white man when small boy on reservation."

"Then you are civilised," Evelyn said naively.

He instantly stiffened as though

insulted. "Stone Eagle not weak, tame, 'good' white man's Indian." He struck his bare, muscular chest with a hard fist. The sharp blow rang through the clearing like a rifle shot. "Strong. Make big medicine. Drive all whites from Comanche hunting lands."

"But they only want to live with you in peace."

"White man's peace is not just," he said, eyes burning with a vast, concentrated bitterness. "Bad for Comanche."

Aware that she was neither qualified nor in a position to debate the issue (not that the proud chieftain would deign to seriously consider the words of a lowly woman captive), Evelyn wisely remained silent and waited for him to state the purpose for his visit; it certainly was not to enquire about her comfort.

"Listen well," Stone Eagle commanded bleakly. "Long as you be plenty good and obey, none will harm you." He gestured to the group around the fire.

"Young Bull has claimed your scalp." Evelyn looked past him to the scar-faced brave watching them across the dancing flames, his face terrible and forbidding, and felt a clutch of fear. "He will not take it — if you mind Stone Eagle and do not stray from his protection."

"I will mind Stone Eagle," Evelyn said, her carefully expressionless face hiding her true intent of doing so only until the chance for escape appeared. Then, dreading the answer, she managed to keep her voice strong as she asked, "What do you want with me?" His flat, dark eyes only stared inscrutably, as if looking straight through her at the scraggly bushes behind her, until she involuntarily squirmed with nervousness.

"You learn in time," Stone Eagle said at last. "Now eat. Sleep. Morning, ride hard." With a rustle of his long feather bonnet he turned and strode back to the fire, leaving Evelyn to ponder with disquietening feelings.

Her mind unleashed a horde of fears, each more terrifying than the last, and she was shocked by the pictures it vividly painted for her fate. Reminding herself that such indulgence was self-defeating, she ended her brooding and turned her thoughts to more practical matters.

Though Evelyn now had no appetite she forced herself to finish the venison, as she did not know when she would be fed again. Clumsily wrapping herself in the blankets, she wriggled about until she was finally in a position for sleep, and lay there, still uncomfortable, feeling the cold seep through the blankets and listening to the guttural voices around the campfire.

She waited, but Stone Eagle must have taken her word, for her guard did not come to bind her more securely for the night. Not that it made any difference. Every muscle ached, and even if she were somehow able to summon the strength to free herself, she was in no condition to escape.

All she could do was try to sleep off her weariness, and then keep herself ready for any unforseen opportunity that might present itself.

Resigned to discomfort, Evelyn huddled on her side and stared up at the full moon above. It appeared much larger and brighter in the mountains, and she felt she could almost reach up and touch it. Thoughts of home came to mind unbidden, starting with the large, soft-four-poster bed in which she used to sleep. Then followed memories of the great white-pillared house, surrounded by wide green fields and white fences . . . the rides over the plantation with her father, brother, and guests . . . quiet afternoon teas . . . and balls, with uniformed men, beautifully gowned women, lilting music, and charming conversations.

Evelyn roused herself from her memories before they became melancholy. She must remain strong, and dared not allow self-pity to make her weak or indecisive. She did not know how or when the moment for escape would come, but she was determined to move quickly when it did. And that meant she must be coolly in control of her emotions. By now Travis had learned of the stagecoach massacre and was on their trail. Should escape prove impossible, then he would rescue her — of that she was certain.

Evelyn permitted herself the luxury of a smile. If only Travis could see her now, eating venison jerky and sleeping on the hard ground, any doubts he might have about her 'frailty' would surely vanish. Her thoughts lingering on Travis, Evelyn finally drifted off to sleep, fitfully at first, and then soundly.

★ ★ ★

In spite of the bleak chill that had replaced the torrid heat of day Travis Dixon was sweat-soaked. He was also running out of wind. His pace had slowed to trotting fifty steps and walking fifty, interspersed by occasional halts to listen sharply and scan his surroundings. The terrain had become wasteland, more rock than sand, with scrubby patches of greasewood and tall stalks of yucca breaking the harsh emptiness before the rolling foothills and mountains beyond. There were now no tell-tale tracks, but the Comanches' lead had probably enabled them to reach the mountains before camping for the night. Taking several deep, ragged breaths, Travis doggedly set off at a trot toward the looming hills.

By the time Travis had covered the half-mile distance a change of wind brought the smell of smoke. Drawing his Colt, he skirted the base of a hill and cautiously crouched in a shadowy nest of rocks. As he had thought, it was not the Comanches' camp.

Three white men were grouped around a near-smokeless campfire in a wide clearing, their horses tethered off on a far side.

Travis did not automatically feel a surge of relief at the sight. Out in the wilderness away from any local law men were free to be as good or bad as they chose; and white or not, strangers were not necessarily always friendly. Still, he needed help, and maybe the men had seen Evelyn and the Comanches. As frontier etiquette said it was not polite (or wise) to blunder into a man's camp without being asked, Travis announced himself.

Instantly the men whirled, one dropping his coffee cup, and jerked their six-guns. "Awright, mister, come ahead on," one man called, squinting into the darkness, "but nice'n slow and with your hands empty."

Travis emerged with his gear, and suspicious eyes and guns remained on him the length of his walk to the fire. "Evening, gents," he said amiably and, keeping his movements casual and unmenacing, dumped his saddlebags and bedroll to the ground. "You can put those guns away. I'm no road agent." He squatted before the fire and warmed his hands.

The man who had first spoken, tall, gaunt-faced, with dark hair and hard, wary eyes, slowly leathered his Colt and the others followed suit. "Where's your horse?" he asked.

"Prairie dog hole. Been walking for some time now."

"This ain't no country to be in without a horse," the man said, and sank down cross-legged across the fire from Travis.

"That's fer sure," the shorter, rat-faced man agreed unnecessarily and gave a snorting chuckle.

"We got none to spare," the big black-bearded man put in quickly.

"Figured as much," Travis said, throwing a lazy glance toward the three horses across the clearing. He felt the men's collective tension and sensed maybe he shouldn't look too closely at the brands, not that he could see them from this distance. He turned his gaze to the coffee pot warming on a grill placed over an edge of the fire. "Coffee sure smells good," he drawled, and felt the tension ease.

"Amos, fetch the man a cup," the obvious leader said to the rat-faced man, who rooted through their utensils and produced another tin cup.

"Here yuh are, red-hot," Amos said, filling the cup and handing it across the fire to Travis.

Travis casually took the cup with his left hand, leaving his gun hand free, and noticed the rat-faced man's beady eyes lingered a shade too long on his bulging saddlebags for idle curiosity. Between sips of strong, scalding coffee he told about his search. The men listened with polite interest, and Travis grimly reminded himself that he couldn't honestly expect strangers to get too worked up over his troubles.

"We seen some Injun signs but that's all," the leader said with a negative shrug.

"We done come from the north," Amos said.

"Northwest," the leader quickly corrected.

"El Paso," the bearded man added clumsily.

"So we wouldn't have crossed trails with your bunch," the leader said, closing the subject.

Travis didn't push it. He figured the men were probably on the dodge, but that was the law's concern. They had not seen Evelyn's party, and that was all he'd wanted to learn.

"You know, you might not find your woman alive," the leader said, obviously steering the conversation back on track, "*if* you even find her at all."

"And then you might not even want her back," the bearded man said with a slight sneer.

Travis tensed, turning cold, narrow eyes on him "Say what you mean," he demanded, dead-flat.

"What ol' Shank means is Injuns ain't much civil to their captives," the leader quickly interjected, filling the harsh silence before things had a chance to turn mean. "She might not have bore up too good under their treatment." He touched the side of his head.

"That's right, Jack," Amos eagerly agreed. "She could be all squirrelly-headed by now."

"You gotta forgive the boys," the leader, now identified as Jack, said in easy apology. "Their mamas sadly neglected their upbringing. They sometimes say things before considering other folks' feelings." He shot both men a steely glance that silenced any contradictions.

"Some folk just naturally have that habit," Travis begrudgingly agreed. It was obvious that neither man would start anything unless told, and their leader was not anxious for trouble. With Kiowas and Comanches on the prowl, it didn't make good sense to start feuding.

"Just so's you won't think too poorly of us, here's what we'll do," Jack said, relaxed. "Come morning we'll take you to the nearest ranch or town, and you can do whatever you've a mind to. How's that?"

"I'd be obliged," Travis replied. They might take him out of his way, but without a horse he would never catch up with Evelyn and her captors.

"Then it's settled," Jack said, his tone overly pleased. He stood and made a broad gesture. "Bed down wherever you like, and we'll git started at first light."

Travis nodded and watched the men drift off to their sleeping area. Amos was grinning like a persimmon-full possum, and Travis decided he'd best sleep light. It was the careful fella who never trusted anybody till he got to know him, and these three didn't inspire much trust. Keeping the fire between him and the men, he wrapped himself in his bedroll. His movement hidden, he eased the Colt from its holster and went to sleep with it in his hand.

5

EVELYN was turned out of her blanket cocoon before the faintest grey appeared in the early morning sky. Her guard closely examined the knots on her bindings, then satisfied that she had made no attempt to loosen them, untied her and dropped a few strips of jerky into her lap before leaving with the blankets. Shivering in the crisp air, she drew her legs up to her body and huddled while watching the Comanches preparing to break camp. The fire was only a dim, reddish glow of dying embers, and the deep, gloomy sky told it was the darkest time just before dawn. She ignored the moving shapes of men and horses and put her chattering teeth to work the tough jerky.

By the time Evelyn had devoured her breakfast the first hint of false dawn was paling the eastern sky. Her guard returned, wordlessly tied her wrists in front of her and drew her up by an arm. At first she could hardly stand, but much of her weariness had been slept away and her youthful body quickly restored itself. She was marched to her waiting horse, helped atop the rawhide and blanket saddle, and her ankles bound. To her welcome surprise the ends of the pony's hackamore were thrust into her hands and she was allowed to control the mount herself.

Stone Eagle trotted up on his decorated Pony and gave her a lengthy, solemn gaze. He and his band were naked to the waist, except for their various ornaments, and Evelyn wondered how they kept warm. Unconcerned by her shivering discomfort, he offered her no wrap and merely said, "Remain near Stone Eagle on this day's journey." With that he kneed his mount ahead, and Evelyn and her guard guided their ponies close behind him. The others straggling in a loose column, the group set off along the mountain trail.

Raised in flat bayou country Evelyn was unaccustomed to heights. The trail, if one could dignify it as such, was only a trace snaking in and out of boulders and stunted greasewood along a ravine, sometimes bearing directly toward the precipice, then swerving and taking them to the very edge of the cliff. It was unsettling in the semi-darkness and she knew it would be positively terrifying in broad daylight. She tried closing her eyes but that only increased her sense of vertigo and she quickly abandoned the idea.

Somewhere close behind a horse's hoof dislodged a large rock. Evelyn heard it strike, bound, hit again, bounce once more, and then only silence followed. Evidently its next landing was so far below that the sound did not reach her. As the trail continued to zigzag, Evelyn had a view of both Stone Eagle and her guard ahead and the rest of the Indians behind her, inching their way along the ledge. They appeared as cautious and fearful as she, and that realisation abruptly dispelled the myth she had built in her mind of Comanche invincibility. They were mere flesh and blood mortals with the same fears as any white man.

To further reduce them to human terms Evelyn mentally pictured Stone Eagle or any of his band alone in New Orleans, where a Comanche would be as lost, frightened and bewildered as she was in this barren country. That amusing thought momentarily diverted her mind from the dangerous trail and brought renewed hope for escape. The opportunity might well come during a moment of hesitation on the trail, and she must not allow her aversion to heights to impede her actions.

All else forgotten, Evelyn determinedly set herself to the task of overcoming that fear.

★ ★ ★

A bright star hung low in the pearl-tinted predawn sky as Travis came hard awake, tensing in his bedroll, prodded by instinct rather than any sound that had penetrated his sleep.

Something was wrong.

He sensed it. Somebody else might dismiss it as just a feeling and nothing more, but he *knew*. He had spent too many years on the frontier to disregard the familiar chill up the ladder of his backbone which came whenever things weren't right.

There was light movement beside him.

Travis turned and saw Amos kneeling above him, large bowie knife raised. Startled by his intended vicitim's sudden awakening, the rat-aced man hesitated — and Travis instantly shot him through the blanket.

The bullet caught Amos under the jaw and somersaulted him backwards in a cloud of smoke and dust.

Kicking free of his bedroll, Travis sat up. Ahead, frozen stock-still by the echoing gunshot, Jack and Shank were back-lit against the dying campfire and greying sky. Jack stood straight up, pistol in hand. Shank clutched a rifle and was bent forward slightly, as if from its weight. Across the clearing the horses shrilled and stamped in their hobbles.

Two shots screamed past Travis' head. He threw himself to one side and, his situation reduced to the simple mathematics of survival, concentrated first on Jack. Holding the Colt's trigger back, he fanned the hammer rapidly. All three shots found their mark.

Each slug hammered Jack backwards, stiff-legged, on his heels. His six-gun discharged into the ground, kicking up a shower of dirt and dust, and then he sprawled flat on his back atop the glowing remnants of the campfire. Arms and legs outflung, he lay unmoving.

A bullet tickled Travis' sleeve, reminding him of Shank. He swung the Colt toward the big man and belly-shot him before he could jack a fresh round into the Winchester's chamber.

Shank gave a deep grunt, folded in the middle and crashed to his knees. Despite his agony he laboriously worked the lever and cocked a bullet into the rifle. Travis aimed at Shank's shaggy head, but the Colt's hammer fell with a harsh click on a faulty shell. He tried again. The pistol was empty. Shank struggled to bring the rifle to bear. Hurling the Colt, Travis went for his knife.

Shank bobbed his head aside and the heavy six-gun harmlessly brushed his hat brim as it flew past. Still, it threw off his aim. Travis drew back his arm and flung the knife.

The blade sank to the hilt in Shank's brawny chest an instant before he fired. His shot fanned Travis' shoulder. Dropping the rifle, he gripped the quivering knife handle in both hands and wrenched it free. With the violent movement he lurched to his feet. Face contorted in rage, the big man brandished the bloody knife and took two staggering steps toward Travis. Then he abruptly pitched forward, loose as a rag doll, and slammed face down in the dirt.

Travis drew a steady breath and his eyes swept the area. Nothing moved except the horses. He now had the camp to himself.

★ ★ ★

The sun rose higher above the vast horizon, its yellow-violet flame chasing dark shadows before it into the hollows of the rising humped mountains.

Having chosen the two best horses (whose muddied-over US brands told that the three men had been Army deserters) and distributed the weapons and supplies evenly between them, Travis was winding his way up a gravelly mountain trail. The Comanches were evidently so confident that no effort had been made to conceal their passage. He judged they had ridden up single

82

file late the previous afternoon or early evening, and most likely they were now well on their way from wherever they had camped for the night. Mountain travel should slow them some, but it would also slow him.

Travis turned in his saddle, cinches creaking against the winded snorts and monotonous clop of the horses' hoofs, and studied the surroundings. Satisfied that he apparently had the trail to himself as far as the eye could see, he begrudgingly halted on a wider, more level spot to let the horses blow and rest for a bit. Winchester in hand, he lowered himself heavily to the ground and stretched his shaky legs. He gave each horse a few handfuls of water from one of the four canteens and drank himself.

Travis paced restlessly, drawing out his wait a few minutes more, and looked out at the desert. The early morning sun softened its harshness and an array of colours brightened the grey drabness with streaks of pink, orange and vermilion. Every time he looked upon the desert he saw something new in its ever-changing terrain. But its seemingly-serene beauty was marred by the knowledge that every living thing out there existed by the death of another less fortunate, and night and day countless unseen life and death battles were constantly waged for survival.

Well, he had his own battle brewing — and the sooner he got at it the better.

Changing horses, Travis hauled himself into the saddle and resumed his ascent. He felt sure he was nearing the campsite and expected to come upon it around each bend of the trail.

An hour later he did.

To his relief there were no signs of a struggle and Evelyn's body was not to be found. The moccasined footprints and sets of pony tracks confirmed that the band were still together; and the smaller imprints of a woman's bare feet told that Evelyn had continued the journey with them. It looked like they had pulled out just before dawn.

Travis now felt a mite better. The fact that Evelyn had survived the night proved the Comanches had plans other than death by torture in store for her. The alternatives were hard but meant life, however hellish. He didn't waste time speculating on their intentions; if things went right he would have Evelyn back before anything could happen.

Travis stalked to the ground-tied horses, chose the fresher mount and, leading the other behind him, rode from the clearing.

* * *

For most of the morning they had climbed higher, as if racing the rising sun, among great rugged heights that Evelyn had first thought impassable. Now, as the sun was nearing its zenith, they were cautiously winding down a devil's staircase of giant, uneven boulders, narrow ledges worn into the age-old rock face, and occasional shaley inclines that promised to slide right out from under them at any moment.

On those forbidding stretches her captors would dismount and make their way on foot, leaving Evelyn to desperately knee-grip and cling to her pony's mane with her bound hands while silently praying it would retain its footing and consigning the Indians to the deepest, fieriest pit in hell for subjecting her to the additional torment. There was no question that the descent was far more unnerving than the ascent.

Noon found them halted on a broad rock shelf overlooking a vast prairie dotted with mesquite, scrub brush and dwarfed oak. Ignoring Evelyn who still sat her horse, the dismounted Comanches were staring off intently at an approaching dust trail. Though small and dim the distant shapes were distinguishable as horsemen loosely grouped around a waggon. Evelyn's breath caught hard in her breast at the realisation they were white men.

Here, at last, was the opportunity she had patiently awaited.

Until now an escape attempt had merely been an absurd flight of fancy. Her captors would immediately come after her. She had no idea which direction to go and knew nothing about concealing her trail — an impossible task anyway while bound on a horse. They would most certainly catch her and possibly even kill her out of hand. At least Young Bull would try. Stone Eagle had warned her, and she was still receiving baleful glances every time her eyes happened to meet those of the scar-faced warrior's.

From the eager sing-song voices Evelyn gathered an attack was under discussion. That meant her escape was vital; only she could warn the unsuspecting men of their danger. She took a guarded look at the trail and was further heartened by what she saw.

Broad enough for two horses abreast, the course wound down in a series of switchbacks to scattered clumps of juniper, oak and pine at the mountain's rocky, sloping base. While it was not as formidable as those she had previously traversed, Evelyn's throat went dry at the harrowing prospect of a headlong dash down the tortuous trail. But there was no choice; lives other than hers depended upon her success.

Evelyn's eyes darted back to the Comanches who, because of her calculated passivity, still disregarded her as the debate raged. She dared not delay a second longer.

Heart pounding she whacked the ends of the hackamore against the pony's neck and, bowling over her startled guard, sent it leaping down the trail at a dead run. Wild howls of surprise went up behind her followed by a mad scramble. She heard only the frenzied tattoo of hoofs and the wind of the breakneck speed roaring in her ears and whipping at her dress and streaming hair.

Seeing his chance to finally obtain

the white squaw's prized yellow scalp, Young Bull was the first mounted. He shouldered his pony through the tangle and galloped off ahead of the others. Aware of his intent, Stone Eagle urgently put his horse in pursuit at a reckless gallop, leaving the rest of the band to straggle after him.

Long hair stinging her face and partially obscuring her vision, Evelyn gave her pony its head and trusted to its sure-footedness. A fall would mean disaster to both on the huge rocks below; still she relentlessly forced the horse on.

A savage yell came from behind her. Though there was little enough time to look where her wildly galloping mount was taking her, Evelyn managed a hasty backward glance.

Not more than fifty yards away rode Young Bull, flourishing his large scalping knife. War bonnet and feathered lance aflutter, Stone Eagle was gaining on him rapidly. They had forged ahead and a considerable gap lay between them and the others who were riding hard behind.

Evelyn turned back; all of her attention was needed to drive her stumbling, faltering pony down the snaking trail. None of the horses had sufficiently rested and her pursuers were at a similar disadvantage. If she could maintain her lead there was every chance of winning freedom.

Hearing Stone Eagle drawing nearer, Young Bull, heels drumming, urged his gasping horse into a desperate flurry of speed. He cared not what plans his chief had for the white woman; he had already claimed her scalp and was not about to be denied it a second time.

Out of the tail of her eye Evelyn saw Young Bull's pony beginning to pull alongside. She jerked her mount to the left and successfully blocked its way, almost forcing horse and rider over the side of the trail. The act only increased his fury. Howling in bloodlust, he again drove his pony forward, slamming its shoulder into her horse's hindquarters and throwing it off stride. Evelyn cried out at the violent impact and pulled back on the hackamore to keep her stumbling animal's head up.

Yelling and slashing, Young Bull was alongside as they swept around a bend. Evelyn ducked low and sideways, evading the flashing blade, and her frightened pony pulled ahead.

They were nearing the base of the mountain, but it no longer represented safety. Unhampered by the twisting trail the scar-faced warrior would easily hack her to pieces on the flat, open plain.

Again they were thundering along neck-in-neck. Young Bull swiped at her, the whisking blade coming so close she could feel the rush of air. Evelyn flinched away and felt the rawhide bite into her bruised ankles as painfully as any knife stroke. Young Bull guided his pony close, his bare leg pressing hers and raised the knife high.

Berserk with fury Stone Eagle smashed

his heels into his frothing pony's salt-encrusted sides, shocking it out of its lethargy of exhaustion, and dropped into a crouch, lance extended.

Heart beating wildly Evelyn cringed, aware she could no longer avoid the deadly blade. Young Bull's painted, scarred face was terrible as he shrieked in triumph.

Abruptly the sound became a gurgling cry. His face contorted in agony and surprise as blood poured out of his open mouth. Evelyn shifted her eyes and saw he was impaled on a feathered lance. Then Stone Eagle's pony burst between them and sent the dying brave's mount staggering over the edge of the trail. Their eerie screams were cut short by the rocks a hundred feet below.

Bloody lance in hand Stone Eagle galloped alongside Evelyn to the foot of the mountain before reaching over and wresting the hackamore ends from her and bringing their exhausted ponies to a halt. Tears of bitter defeat welled in Evelyn's eyes, blurring Stone Eagle's harsh features, yet she found herself growing calm in a sense of fatalism.

She had tried and failed — and now she must pay the price for her transgression. She only hoped that death would be swift and painless.

6

THE rag-tail hunters were planning on nooning on the other side of the folded hills ahead, out of sight from anyone roaming the prairie. The twelve men knew that bands of hostiles were plundering the area, but so far luck had been with them. If it continued to hold they would be safe in Brackettville by week's end with their precious waggonload of furs and buffalo hides. After over three months in the wilds all were looking forward to the journey's end, and spirits grew with every passing mile.

Raised in the arid Llano River country the Waller boys, Andy and Lucas, were the only true frontiersmen, the others being scions of wealthy Eastern families who had come West on a lark, for profit and adventure. Larcenous, quarrelsome illiterates, the brothers were tolerated because of their knowledge of the country and its savage inhabitants. They, in turn, tolerated the damnyankees because of their money.

Tall, wolf-lean and two years older, Lucas prided himself on having the most 'horse sense' and fed his self-esteem at his burly, heavy-faced brother's expense. That habit had a less than endearing effect on Andy and was often a source of friction between them. At the moment they were lagging behind to keenly survey their back-trail and Andy was again wistfully scheming how to keep the furs for themselves. The much-belaboured subject once more compelled Lucas to irritably become the voice of reason.

"I done told you the carpetbaggers would tax that stuff sky-high if we showed up anywhere in the state all by our lonesomes. But they ain't gonna do that to their own kind. We need this lot. Can't you git that through your thick skull?"

"We could 'light a shuck' for Sante

Fe and sell 'em there, away from the stinkin', taxin' carpetbaggers."

"Sure, fightin' Kiowas, Comanches, Apaches, Navajos and Mes-can *banditos* all the way — not to mention our own bunch of renegades." Lucas gave a derisive snort. "That is somethin' I just can't hardly wait to git started doin'!"

"Now don't you go to devillin' me again, Lucas," Andy cautioned, holding up a hamhock fist.

"Then you hush up that nonsense till you got somethin' sensible to say," Lucas shot back, undaunted.

Andy screwed up his face in thought, clearly a painful task for someone used to solving problems by brute strength. Hard cash was difficult for any Southerner to come by in the defeated South, and he was reluctant to let the opportunity slip through his fingers. Before a solution could come to him excited shouts went up from the lead riders, and he and Lucas twisted in their saddles.

Dust from the other horsemen and the heavily-loaded waggon obscured their vision, but something mighty important seemed to be going on. The brothers exchanged questioning scowls, then Lucas gave an easy shrug.

"Reckon we'd best git on up there and see what all the fuss is about."

Yeah," Andy agreed. "Maybe them dudes come across a real fierce varmint — like another horned toad?"

Lucas grinned as he recalled the tenderfoots' first encounter with one of the menacing-looking but harmless lizards. Hollering and hopping around like they were in the middle of a red ant hill, the young Easterners had shot the 'rattlesnake' to bits, while the Waller boys nearly split a gut laughing. Afterwards, they had delighted in not allowing the uppity, red-faced Yankees to live down the humiliating incident for several weeks.

The two gigged their horses into a canter and joined the riders halted ahead of the waggon, just shy of a broad passage between two rocky hills. They drew rein beside the party's leader, New Yorker Ronald Turner, a fastidious young man who continually behaved as though they were gaming on his family's Long Island estate. His usually aloof, aristocratic features now shone with excitement as he gestured toward a sloping, sparsely wooded area at the base of the mountain a short distance beyond the hills.

"Look, Waller, a white woman!"

Lucas followed Turner's waving arm and immediately tensed at the sight of a blonde woman in a badly torn dress gagged and lashed to a prominent cedar. "Yeah, it sure enough looks like one," he drawled, with a casualness he did not feel, and threw a meaning glance at Andy.

"Guess we ain't noonin' here," the big man said dryly, attempting to match his brother's casualness.

"How can you think of food?" Turner demanded, shocked by his apparent

98

callousness. "We can't leave her. She's alive!"

"Too far to tell for sure," Lucas said quietly, his eyes warily drifting about the woman's area. "Could be an Injun's hid behind that tree, moving her body hisself . . ."

"It's been done before," Andy stated.

"I tell you she *is* alive," Turner repeated emphatically. Several others in the group agreed.

"We ain't got no choice," Lucas said, allowing only his eyes to move as he surveyed the hills before them. "They's Injuns all around, just waitin' for us to go to her like a bunch of little high-bred gentlemen."

"Right as rain," Andy put in.

"Now let's ease on outta here," Lucas advised, "and hope to hell they don't wantta fight when they see we're wise to their tricks."

The prudent suggestion didn't sit well with Turner and his men, and they made it known in no uncertain terms.

"She has been left to die," Turner stubbornly persisted. "There probably isn't an Indian within miles."

"Then you just go right ahead on up there and find out," Lucas said with a sweep of his hand.

Turner suddenly felt a moment of indecision as all eyes were upon him. He disliked the two unwashed hirelings and would like nothing better than to prove them craven. Yet if they were right he would be riding to his death. Then again, a helpless woman would die needlessly if they were wrong. It was a damnable dilemma, and he wished they had never seen the woman. He had stupidly played into Waller's hands, allowing him to effectively call his bluff in front of everyone. He had been given a choice, and the decision was solely his. Though Turner had never been a soldier, he now painfully understood the loneliness of command.

Honour and family pride (rather than Christian charity) finally made the decision for him. It was far better to risk uncertain death than leave and spend the rest of his life haunted by guilt — or fear that a comrade would one day confess their shameful secret, in the demented belief it would absolve a tormented conscience, and bring about disgrace *and* disinheritance.

"Very well, Waller," Turner said in utter contempt, drawing himself ramrod-straight in the saddle, "I shall do exactly that." He started his horse forward at a slow walk, eyes cautiously scanning what lay ahead, and secretly hoped that his display of courage would inspire others to follow.

None did.

★ ★ ★

From her vantage point halfway up the slope, Evelyn saw the lone horseman leave the waiting group. She wanted to cry an urgent warning but was prevented by the crude 'Comanche bridle'; a bulky strip of buckskin loosely wrapped around the middle

101

of a stick, its ends tied with thongs knotted at the back of her head. Any attempt to scream would cause the buckskin to unravel, filling her mouth and strangling her, and she was forced to constantly clench the 'bit' in her teeth in order to breathe.

When dragged to the tree by four warriors, Evelyn had at first feared she was being prepared for torture. Wrists fastened up behind her, forcing her body forward on straining tiptoes, rawhide wrapping her waist, ankles tied on either side of the trunk, she had grimly awaited slow execution. But to her confusion the insidious gag was added (she had heard that Indians usually delighted in competing to see who could wring the loudest screams from their victims) and the braves had withdrawn. The reason had become clear when the Comanches spread in a wide semicircle and concealed themselves behind rocks and trees.

Stone Eagle had set a trap for the

white men — and she was the alluring bait.

Through the broad gap between the hills, Evelyn had watched the dust clouds mark the hunting party's plodding progress across the heat-waved prairie. Every second had seemed to stretch to eternity. Again and again, she had struggled to exhaustion, supple muscles standing out in clear profile, until finally forced to accept the futility of her act. Slowly the blurred shapes had become individual men and horses, and then they were halted a hundred yards ahead, shouting and pointing up at her.

Tumbled mane of golden hair partially concealing her face, Evelyn now tensely watched the single rider's wary approach. He was within the jaws of the trap, but the hidden Comanches patiently held their fire, evidently waiting for him to beckon the others to join him. Evelyn wildly shook her head and, disregarding the many hurts to her straining body, once more fought her rawhide bindings. She knew that she was risking a Comanche bullet or arrow, but she was determined not to be a passive participant in the ambush.

Still the rider came steadily forward.

Evelyn desperately hoped he had not misinterpreted her movements as those of great relief and excitement at being rescued by white men. Eyes large and fearful, she continued to watch the horseman.

★ ★ ★

Ronald Turner was unsure of the exact reason for the woman's struggles, but he had already sensed danger around him. Even his horse's ears were pricked up and the animal was skittish. He bitterly cursed his bravado.

'Death before Dishonour' was a foolish, outmoded sentiment. There were countless places where one could flee to escape the stigma and, if enterprising, amass new wealth. Besides, there was no guarantee any of his cowardly party would ever speak of this day, even amongst themselves. Also, for all he knew, the woman was a trollop, and certainly not worth the risk of one's life.

The thought that any instant might bring a slug or arrow from an unseen savage lifted the hair on the nape of his neck and gave him a cold chill. Though he saw nothing suspicious he knew that Indians were masters in the art of concealment. Some might even be right out in plain sight, motionless, blending in with the surroundings like desert animals. They could be close by and he would not see them until there was movement — and then it would be too late.

Suddenly, with startling clarity, the icy realisation that he would die swept through Turner. The woman be damned, he could not go a single yard farther. He desperately wanted to live, and his only hope of survival lay behind him. It might already be too late, but he must try to extricate himself from the unseen trap into which he had blundered.

Yielding to panic, Turner viciously bridled his mount around and slapped his heels into its flanks. Anxious as its rider to leave the place, the horse sprang forward and broke into a wild run. Almost simultaneously came the flat slap of bows and four whistling arrows thudded into his back and chest.

And Ronald Turner was instantly relieved of all of life's mundane responsibilities to honour and family.

7

THE Waller boys already had their Henry repeaters resting across their saddle bows and were ready when Turner's horse, stirrups flapping wildly, came galloping out from between the two hills with a horde of howling Comanches close behind.

"Aw, hell, I knowed it," Andy groaned and spat a brown stream of tobacco juice before bringing his rifle to his shoulder.

"Fire together," Lucas called. "Then we'll make tracks before they can regroup." Unfortunately, no one was listening. Unnerved by the terrifying Comanche war cries, the big city boys broke and scattered every which way.

Rapidly levering their rifles, the Wallers hosed bullets at the oncoming Comanches, bringing the lead warriors and horses tumbling down into the others' path, and succeeded in slowing the charge.

"Every man for hisself," Andy bellowed, "and the devil takes the hindmost." With that he jerked his mount around and put the spurs to it. Lucas was right beside him and they headed after the rattling, dust-spewing waggon racing back out onto the prairie.

Seeing the white men's disorder, the thundering Comanches split into bands and gave chase. The fleeing men were quickly overtaken and small individual battles raged before the hills, with each warrior trying to outdo the other in bravery. But there were scant honours to be garnered from the slaughter of frightened, inexperienced young men. A few died well though, blasting bucks from their ponies at point-blank range before being dragged from their saddles, but most were brutally dispatched without having fired a shot. More than one still retained a flicker of life when the scalping knives finally came into play.

Intent on rescuing the waggon and its goods, the Waller brothers spared no backward glances at the inevitable massacre. Shots and arrows sought them as a dozen shrieking braves came in mad pursuit. Aided by poor marksmanship and the waggon's trail of thick, billowing dust, the two hunkered lower in their saddles and spurred on.

Then a well-placed shot shattered the driver's spine and hurled him head first from the seat. He sprawled limply onto the waggontongue and hung for a long moment, before a deep rut violently jolted him beneath the waggon.

Seeing the driverless waggon, Andy drove his horse relentlessly to catch the runaway team. He was alongside the driver's seat and preparing to make the transfer when the opposite wheels slammed against the side of a huge, half-buried rock and splintered loudly. The waggon shuddered and collapsed, lop-sided, its whole right side ploughing up earth, rocks and dust as the galloping team slowed and strained in their traces. Cussing a blue streak, Andy plopped back down in the saddle and begrudgingly abandoned the disabled waggon to his gaining pursuers.

The screeching Comanches quickly halted the dragging waggon and eagerly laid claim to its goods. Still caught up in the heat of the chase, four warriors continued after the escaping white men and their fresher ponies soon put them within rifle range. Knees guiding their mounts, the three with rifles began firing with both hands while the fourth brandished his lance and hoped to still be in on the kill if the white men or their horses were brought down.

Tearing along side by side, Andy and Lucas spread wide as bullets peppered the air around them. Neither troubled to return fire; every bullet would be precious should they be forced to make a stand. Their slobbering, staggering horses threatened to turn that unsettling prospect into reality. They covered another half-mile, and then Andy's luck ran out.

The big man gave a startled yell as his horse abruptly went down, pinning his left leg before he could kick his feet free of the stirrups. For a long moment he was helpless to move, then, one ear pressed to the ground, the vibrating sound of drumming hoofbeats roused him from his stupor. He shoved himself up to a half-sitting position, saw the distant oncoming Comanches and, hollering his name, frantically looked about for Lucas.

Lucas reined in and turned back to see his brother's distress. Had it been one of them arrogant Yankees he would have kept right on going, but the iron tie of blood held him back. Kin was kin — and, like 'em or not, a body just didn't desert kinfolks to the mercy of Indians. Letting loose a wild Rebel yell, he booted his horse forward.

Heartened that his brother was coming to his aid, Andy grabbed the saddle's pommel and cantle and, shoulders bent, began straining to raise the horse's dead weight from his trapped leg. Bullets whipped about waspishly, but he did not cease his efforts. Several slugs whammed into the carcass and Andy swore like a mule-skinner as the violent impacts caused the saddle to buck loose from his grip.

Lucas jerked in his mount, brought the Henry to his shoulder and took aim at the leader of the pack, well out ahead of the others. The warrior was swaying from side to side as he came, working his rifle. Sighting on the brave's stationary waist, Lucas let go a round.

Victory cry becoming an agonised shriek, the brave spun from his pony, bounced and lay writhing, gut-shot, his hip shattered. The other two bucks with rifles veered and charged toward Lucas, leaving the third to easily dispatch the downed white man with his lance.

No longer hampered by flying bullets

Andy again wrestled mightily with the saddle. Sweat trickled down his broad forehead, stinging and blurring his eyes, as he laboured, desperately aware of the approaching rider. Using only the strength of his brawny forearms and shoulders, the big man slowly lifted the dead animal . . . an inch . . . then two . . . and slid his leg free. He was not a moment too soon. The screaming warrior was bearing down on him, crouched, lance extended.

Andy threw a wild glance about for Lucas. He was in time to see a warrior blasted backwards from his pony. Then, both out of shells, Lucas and the second warrior came whooping at each other. Regardless of the outcome, Andy could expect no help in time. He lurched to his feet and stood facing the shrieking, paint-smeared brave.

At the last second Andy twisted aside, grabbed the lance in both hands and gave a powerful yank. The warrior came somersaulting off his pony and slammed to a stop on his back. Moving with surprising speed for a big man, Andy was onto the stunned brave and drove the raised lance down at his chest before he could rise. The tremendous two-handed thrust impaled the warrior to the ground, kicking and writhing like a speared fish, his intense rage momentarily surpassing the agony of death.

"C'mon now, Injun," Andy coaxed, his face expressing pure pleasure, "holler good for me." He effortlessly dug the lance tip deeper into the sodden earth beneath the flopping brave and wiggled the shaft about, eliciting a horrid scream before his victim gave a mighty shudder and lay still. Grinning, Andy released the lance then stepped back and remarked aloud, "Anybody says Injuns don't scream their hurt just like white folks does is a damned liar." A distant pistol crack interrupted his gloating and made him whirl in Lucas' direction.

Lucas and the remaining warrior had unhorsed each other. Tomahawk raised, the Indian was staggering backwards from Lucas' prone form. He caught himself, started forward. A second slug halted him in mid-stride and threw him to the ground. Lucas scrambled up, shot the brave again to be sure he stayed down, then looked over and waved to Andy.

Relieved, Andy waved back and set about collecting his gear while Lucas rounded up his horse. The spooky Indian mustangs had taken off and, though neither was muchly fond of the idea, Andy was forced to climb aboard behind Lucas.

"We sure as hell can't outrun nobody with your big, fat self a-turnin' my horse into a swayback," Lucas grumbled.

"Ain't no Injuns houndin' us," Andy snapped. "And none will, when they git a look at what we done to this bunch."

"I'll remember them words whilst

they's liftin' our scalps," Lucas sneered.

"Aw, quit bellyachin' and let's git."

There was no time to waste on bickering so Lucas begrudgingly allowed Andy the last word and pushed the horse deeper into the prairie.

★ ★ ★

Unwillingly, Evelyn had viewed the battle until it mercifully spread out behind the intervening hills. Still, the sounds had reached her, conjuring in her imagination even more horrid scenes than those she had witnessed. Finally the firing had ceased, replaced for a time by Comanche victory cries, and then silence. Except for an occasional warrior galloping past the break in the hills, Evelyn would have guessed she had been deserted. However pleasant, at first, that thought brought little comfort.

Alone and helpless, she might well die from thirst and exposure before anyone happened to find her. And there was no assurance it would not be another party of Indians instead of Travis. Evelyn still refused to abandon hope that he would come for her, but after the hunters' massacre, what were his chances of success?

Drumming hoofs intruded on her pessimism and Evelyn went rigid at the sight of Stone Eagle and a small band approaching. They halted around Turner's arrow-filled body and begun an argument over his scalp. One brave was granted the honour, and Evelyn's view was thankfully obstructed by the milling men and horses. Then Stone Eagle pointed his bloody spear tip and three braves whipped their ponies toward her. Hands curling into tight fists, long nails digging into her palms, Evelyn watched as they leaped from their mounts and scrambled up the steep incline.

Had her time come, now that she had served Stone Eagle's purpose?

They reached her and she froze in alarm as their knives came out.

Relief streamed through her as the blades harmlessly severed her gag and the rawhide imprisoning her to the tree. Wrists left tied behind her, Evelyn was roughly hurried down the slope between two braves. Her guard, dripping scalp dangling from his waist, rode up with her pony and she was placed on its back, her ankles again firmly tied.

As Evelyn and the band rode out from between the hills she saw the widely scattered carnage and averted her eyes to the line of horses, both those of the white men and dead Comanches, heavily laden with furs and hides. The ambush had provided scalps and profits which would further raise Stone Eagle's esteem in the eyes of his followers, and perhaps that was the reason he had spared her? But on remembering his brief talk, Evelyn sensed it was something more. She was important to him, so much so that he had even killed Young Bull to protect her from harm.

What purpose would she ultimately serve?

Evelyn was still pondering that question when the Comanches briskly resumed their trek and, skirting the hills, entered the vast prairie.

8

AFTER they were sure the Comanches had safely departed, Andy and Lucas cautiously circled back to the massacre site to see what might be salvaged. The first pickings were mighty poor, yielding only a few silver coins dropped in haste.

"Damn Injuns ain't content with scalps, horses and weapons no more," Andy complained, jingling three silver dollars in a meaty palm. "Now they gotta rob a man's pockets as well — not to mention all them furs."

"It's the damn Comancheros' doin'," Lucas said, straightening up from a nearby penniless, half-naked corpse. "Injuns know them white renegade sumbitches will take just about anythin' in trade."

"Only ones gonna do right well

is them filthy buzzards," Andy said disgustedly and motioned up at the dark circling flock impatiently dipping lower as their appetites grew.

"Yeah," Lucas said in equal disgust. "We'd best finish up pronto and clear out, before they bring some curious, unwelcome folk — like Kiowas and such."

Andy heaved to his feet, thumbed his hat off his broad forehead and surveyed the other widely strewn bodies. "It's downright unthoughtful of them Yankees not to git kilt together, all nice and neat-like."

"They always was a bother," Lucas remarked.

Leaving the two corpses where they lay, the Wallers trudged off and continued their grisly work. By the time they came to the last man, Ronald Turner, the brothers were in better spirits, having scraped together two silver watches, a silver cigar case and almost forty dollars in folding money, evidently considered worthless paper by the Comanches. Turner's pockets only turned up a few coins, and sent Andy into another dark tirade about Indians and Comancheros.

"Hush your big mouth and look up yonder," Lucas interrupted, pointing toward the mountain trail.

"Injun?" Andy enquired, squinting up at the distant horseman winding down the mountain.

"Sits his horse up straight, like a white man," Lucas replied. "Injuns is always hunched over."

"That fella's leading an extra horse," Andy said and threw a crab look to Lucas. "Reckon he could be persuaded to part with it?"

"Could be," Lucas said casually. "Besides, a man can only ride one horse at a time."

"That's a sure enough fact," Andy said. They exchanged larcenous grins and stood watching the rider slowly make his way down from the mountain.

★ ★ ★

122

The gathering vultures had alerted Travis to the massacre even before he saw the distant broken waggon and a few of the bodies sprawled beyond the foothills. After rounding a bend he was able to see two men standing near a dead man in the wide area before the sloping base of the mountain. Only one reins-tied horse could be seen, and he figured that had something to do with the wide grins and friendly waves from the coarse twosome. He pulled rein a short distance away and let the horses blow. Still grinning, the pair ambled forward to palaver. Travis hooked a leg over the saddle horn, tilted back his hat brim and watched them approach, his seemingly easy manner belying his suspicion.

The three howdied, made introductions and exchanged tales, the Wallers looking pictures of true sorrow at the deaths of 'them poor Yankee boys'. Encouraged, Travis pressed the men about Evelyn.

"We didn't see her close up," Lucas

said. "But if'n she's a 'looker' like you say, there ain't much fear of them doin' her. Comanches got no qualms about marryin' or takin' to mate a beautiful white woman."

"'Course, them they don't choose is made work-slaves and whippin'-girls for any old squaw what needs a helper, or got an unhealthy dislike for whites," Andy cut in.

"But Comanches also likes to trade," Lucas continued. "Whole passels of white gals has disappeared for ever below the border in Old Sonora as concubines of rich Mes-can dons, or no-account *bandido jefes*."

Andy nodded. "Some's even ended up in the *jacals* of Mescalero and Chiricahua Apache chiefs way out west in Arizona Territory."

So far the men weren't saying anything that Travis hadn't heard before, and he was waiting for the subject to get around to his spare horse. But then the conversation got real interesting.

"They's more'n likely headin' for the 'Valley of Tears' to do some tradin'," Lucas said.

Until then Travis had been solely intent on catching the Comanches on the trail and had not even much thought to their destination, other than some isolated tribal campsite. Now he had a very unsettling feeling that Lucas was right.

Since the early days of Texas unscrupulous men of varied nationalities, known as Comancheros, had traded with the Comanches for stolen goods, livestock and captives (whom were often callously ransomed back to their families), and eagerly encouraged the continuous raids for their own profit.

The meetings were first left to chance, then regular rendezvous were set, not only in Texas but Mexico and New Mexico Territory, and Kiowas, Apaches and other bands soon joined in. Whenever the Cavalry or Texas Rangers raided a meeting place others would spring up. The most infamous — and yet undiscovered spot — was the Valley of Tears, so named because even the hardened Comancheros were moved by the weeping of captive white mothers as their children were torn from them and parcelled out to different bands.

"That's where our furs and hides is a-goin', too," Andy said and spat in disgust.

"Either of you happen to know where to find this Valley of Tears?" Travis enquired.

"Rumours put it somewheres around the Rio Grande," Lucas replied. He shrugged and added, "Probably across on the Mes-can Rio Bravo side of the river?"

"Reckon I'll find out soon enough," Travis said idly.

"You still fixin' to go on?" Andy asked in surprise.

"Soon as the horses have their second wind."

Lucas studied Travis for a thoughtful

moment. "How'd you like company?"

"What?" Andy shouted, saving Travis a response.

Dividing his gaze between Andy and Travis, Lucas calmly explained. "Them Comanches got things we all want — and three of us would stand a better chance of gittin' 'em back."

"They can keep them damn furs," Andy said emphatically.

"You been itchin' to lay hold of 'em," Lucas reminded pointedly. "Now that we finally got a clear title you up and change your tune."

"But I weren't plannin' to fight no mess of Injuns and Comancheros to git 'em."

"I swear, Andy, you ain't never gonna amount to nothin' with that kinda disposition."

"Before you boys start squabbling," Travis interjected, "I don't rightly know that I want you along."

"What do you mean by that?" Lucas asked, confused.

You sayin' we ain't fit to ride

with you?" Andy demanded, suddenly belligerent.

"Nothing personal," Travis said easily, trying to soothe ruffled feathers, "but I might do better alone."

"You're refusin' our help?" Lucas asked incredulously.

Travis motioned over to the scalped body a short distance behind the men. You two weren't much help to him and his party."

"They was damn fools what wouldn't listen to common sense," Andy said defensively.

"You fought Injuns before, just like us," Lucas said reasonably, "and there's the difference. We can use each other."

"I know one of you can use a horse."

"And you think that's the only reason we wantta go with you, huh?" Lucas said scornfully.

"Good a reason as any. Then after a few miles you two would get lost."

"We got money to buy that horse," Lucas said.

"Then we could do as we pleased."

"Its not for sale."

"Now that's downright stingy," Andy said, eyeing Travis hard.

Lucas motioned for Andy to be silent and continued to press his case. "With or without your extra horse, we's goin' after our furs."

"Damn right," Andy said, his mind now changed by Travis' rejection.

"We'll be followin' the same trail," Lucas said, "and there's no tellin' what all we might meet up with along the way. Once we git where we're goin we don't hafta stick together unless it's agreed on. Now that's fair enough, ain't it?"

Travis considered Lucas' logic and had to admit it made sense. "All right, but let's get one thing straight," he said flatly. "I'm making a loan of my spare horse. You fellas decide to quit at any time, and it stays with me. That's final — and there'll be no discussion."

Lucas saw his determination and glanced to Andy. You heard the man's

129

terms. It's your choice?"

Andy hesitated, sizing up Travis, then spat a stream of tobacco juice and gave a broad shrug. "Reckon that's fair enough."

"Then mount up," Travis said. "We've burned enough daylight standing around talking."

★ ★ ★

The Comanches were as yet making no attempt to cover their way, which was so clearly marked by the deep hoofprints of the heavily-loaded pack animals that even an Eastern city slicker could easily follow them. Their southwesterly course appeared to confirm Lucas' guess that they were heading for the Rio Grande, and the mysterious Valley of Tears.

Keeping a steady gait, Travis and the Wallers travelled on in near silence for what was left of the afternoon. Several times they paused to rest their mounts and study both their back-trail and what lay ahead. Though Travis still held little confidence in what exactly the back-bush country brothers would do when they finally came upon the Comanches, he hoped the time would come before they reached the Valley of Tears. Despite their greed they might balk at entering the Indian and Comanchero camp. He had no definite plan now, mostly it would depend on the lay of the land when the Comanches were sighted. Three men with repeating rifles could make a deadly ambush; then again, the situation might call for stealthily entering a sleeping camp and retrieving Evelyn and the men's furs.

Dusk came, lengthening and thickening the shadows, and the separating distance still remained wide, with not even the faintest distant dust cloud ahead to betray the Comanches' position. The saddle-weary men halted in a small gully filled with mesquite, palo verde and smoke trees, collected dry wood and heated beans and coffee over a smokeless fire, to accompany their meal of jerky and hardtack.

Afterwards, they buried the glowing coals and brushed over the ground, eliminating all traces of the cook fire. Experienced frontiersmen, they then cautiously travelled a few miles farther before making camp for the night, just in case someone had spotted their fire.

Once again Travis rolled up in his blanket with his Colt in hand. He didn't exactly fear an attack by the Wallers, but a change of mind. And damned if he was going to let Andy slip off during the night with the spare horse.

9

NIGHT passed uneventfully. The prairie subtly stirred with life as its nocturnal inhabitants emerged to forage for survival. A swooping hawk screeched and its dying prey squealed briefly. A coyote complained to the moon and set off a chorus of sharp, eerie howls from the rest of the pack. Once Travis awakened to distant pounding hoofs as a group of horsemen tore across the plain. Gripping the Colt he tensely waited, but no one approached the brush-hidden campsite.

Travis rose at the crack of dawn to find both Wallers snoring soundly and rousted them out of their bedrolls. Andy was dark and sullen as they wolfed down a hastily prepared breakfast, but Lucas cheerfully made light of his brother's mood.

"Andy's always as personable as an ol' sore-tailed cat till he's had his second cup of coffee." Lucas refilled the big man's empty cup. "There you go. Just stick your snout in that." Andy grunted meaninglessly and guzzled the steaming brew.

Travis wondered if the cold light of morning had brought second thoughts and prepared for a confrontation with the big man. It didn't come, but neither did the coffee improve Andy's disposition any.

They were soon in the saddle, and again picked up the Comanches' trail. Several miles along they found the tracks of six unshod horses crossing those of the Comanches, and reckoned they belonged to the riders they'd heard during the night. The men rode on but saw no signs that the passing Indians had changed their course to follow the Comanches.

Morning wore on, and they finally came upon the Comanches' night camp. The departing tracks were about six hours' old, and the party still appeared unconcerned about hiding their trail.

"They's still makin' for the Rio," Lucas commented.

"Probably done crossed long ago," Andy sourly speculated. "Goin' by how they been pushin' their horses."

Travis glumly saw his hope of overtaking the Indians before they reached the Valley of Tears steadily vanishing. Determined not to voice a note of disappointment that might encourage Andy's desertion, he said stoically, "Then we'd best do some pushing too."

He led off at a fast trot, saddle leather creaking, bit-chains jingling, and the men followed.

★ ★ ★

At mid-morning Evelyn and the Comanches halted on the bank of a silt-laden river dotted with sand-bars while their thirsty horses drank. They had travelled almost continuously since false dawn, and she welcomed the brief reprieve from the long, racking ride.

Since her failed escape she was no longer allowed to guide her horse and her arms were constantly kept fastened behind her back. Other than that discomfort she had not been punished for breaking her word. Stone Eagle was not of a forgiving nature, and she knew that kindness was not the reason for his leniency. Before curious speculation could again nag her mind, the chief glanced over at her and broke his austere silence.

"Mexico," he announced, pointing his feathered lance at the desolate land across the river, and prodded his pony into the water. One after another the braves followed his lead.

Evelyn's first reaction was surprise that the famous Rio Grande boundary was not the wide, raging river she had always imagined. But it was quickly replaced by the realisation that she was entering an alien land and might well vanish permanently from her own country's society. Her thoughts were disrupted by the shock of cool water about her bound ankles as the river rose above her plunging mount's belly.

The Comanches gave their horses their heads, letting them pick their own footing through the current, while Evelyn's pony was pulled along behind her guard. Evelyn vainly wished for the use of her hands as she was splashed repeatedly by the wallowing horses. She was almost as drenched as the ponies by the time they scrambled up the crumbling bank, dirt spilling after them, and paused to await the floundering, heavily-loaded pack animals. Then they rode toward a nearby mountain range, and Evelyn took a backward look at the Rio Grande and wondered if she would ever cross it again — and under what circumstances?

An hour later they were into the mountains, entering through a narrow canyon that climbed swiftly between two craggy peaks. They were slowed by the rocky, broken ground, but Stone Eagle pressed forward as fast as the horses could manage without stumbling over the ruts and loose rocks. At times the canyon became so narrow one could touch both walls at once, and the party was forced to drop back into single file. Finally the long, stone corridor walls moved farther apart and the twisting trail became perfectly straight.

By noon they emerged from the canyon's shadowed depths into the bright sunlight and rode across a wide, grass-spotted valley. On finally reaching the far end of the valley a high barrier rose before them. The Comanches flogged their ponies up a steeply winding slope of the arroyo and onto the top of a broad mesa. For another hour they pushed on, then a small valley opened beneath them. The route down was less strenuous but still had Evelyn frantically clamping her aching legs around her pony's heaving flanks and wishing she could cling to its mane.

On reaching the bottom they rested briefly, the braves dismounting while Evelyn was left sitting her horse. Then they rode straight ahead toward another seemingly impassable rocky barrier instead of making for the open end of the valley. Evelyn was dreading another hard scramble up a steep slope, but as they drew nearer a wide passage took shape in the high granite mountain.

They entered the defile and, cooled by its shadows, followed its relatively straight course for several hundred yards before coming out into a broad, level valley, green with tall grass and ringed by sheer, towering walls. A clear running stream bisected the valley and served as a boundary for two uniquely different Indian villages scattered along its banks: conical skin tepees and round-topped, grass-thatched wicki-ups, wood-framed and covered by canvas on one side.

Evelyn stared in awe at her first Indian villages and their swart inhabitants, then noticed the huge herds of grazing livestock farther out in the valley. Cries of welcome went up from the skin lodge village. Stone Eagle spoke to her guard, who then handed him her pony's lead rope and galloped ahead of the war party. Evelyn guessed that he had been sent ahead to spread the news of Stone Eagle's victories and ensure a proper hero's greeting. Sure enough, Stone Eagle delayed until the buck had reached the village and was animatedly riding down the long lines of white or tan-coloured tepees before slowly starting forward, tall and stately, at the head of his band.

Well over a hundred Comanches, mostly men, were eagerly gathered about the lodges by the time they entered the camp. Evelyn noted that the other Indians across the stream, clad in faded shirts, breech clouts and high-legged moccasins, their hair bound back on their foreheads by bandannas, paid scant attention to their arrival. Forgetting her dishevelled appearance, she first gawked in open curiosity at her surroundings, then became aware of the hostile, Mongol faces and, refusing to be intimidated, defiantly drew her weary body as proudly erect as that of their chief. The victorious group dwindled as warriors dropped out at individual lodges and soon only Evelyn and Stone Eagle were left.

They rode to the end of the village where her guard stood watching four squaws in the midst of erecting a tepee beside a shady grove of Spanish oaks. While the men talked, Evelyn looked on in fascination as the construction continued uninterrupted. Four poles, joined together near the top, served as a base and eight others were stacked around to make the tepee roughly circular at the bottom. Evelyn frowned, bewildered, as the women deftly tied a large skin, stretching from about six feet to the ground where it was turned under at the bottom, to the inside of the poles. But it became clear that a tepee was actually double-walled as soon as the squaws began attaching the outer covering. Then the men claimed Evelyn's attention.

Her guard severed the thong connecting her ankles and dragged her from the pony. He allowed her to topple over as her unsupportive legs gave way, and the jarring impact momentarily drove the breath from her body. Dropping to a knee, he quickly cut the rawhide from her wrists and arms, then rose and led her pony away. Too weak to rise, Evelyn was left to painfully chafe the circulation back into her numb limbs.

Stone Eagle summoned one of the squaws from her work and spoke authoritatively in their sing-song language. The thickset, middle-aged woman's dark eyes were full of hatred as they swept over the prone captive.

"Buffalo Woman speaks white man's tongue some," Stone Eagle solemnly informed Evelyn. "Obey all she says. She is free to beat you if you do not." The woman's stoic nod and grunt indicated that she would relish the opportunity. Stone Eagle pointed toward the stream with his lance. "Go. Wash. You are dirty long time. New dress will await you."

Evelyn pushed herself up onto a hip with an elbow and glanced about. A bath would be heaven, but it meant doing so in full view of the village. Looking up at Stone Eagle, she firmly shook her head. The squaw glowered and took a threatening step forward. The chief halted her with a sharp command and stared down at Evelyn.

"None in the village will harm you. Now, go!" He turned his pony and rode back to the village with her previous guard.

Buffalo Woman gave Evelyn a none too gentle nudge in the midriff with a moccasined foot and pointed to the stream. So far Evelyn had been spared torture or any real abuse, but that would quickly change if she persisted in disobedience. Managing her best haughty expression, she drew herself to her feet as gracefully as possible.

It was wasted on Buffalo Woman. No sooner did Evelyn gain her feet than a savage shove sent her reeling to the edge of the bank.

"Dress off," the squaw commanded.

Hoping to delay the inevitable, Evelyn reached behind her back and slowly picked at the dress fastenings. That too was a futile gesture. Buffalo Woman impatiently slapped Evelyn's hands away and ripped the dress down the back. Before Evelyn could recover from her surprise the woman's strong fingers dragged the soiled garment down her body and let it fall in a tumbled heap about her ankles, leaving her standing there stark naked. Then another vicious shove sent her floundering out into the knee-deep current.

Evelyn quickly submerged all but her head beneath the cold water. The squaw gestured for her to wash and stood sulkily waiting, arms crossed. Evelyn took petty delight in luxuriating in the water until the woman snatched a stick and was about to wade in after her. She made a grand show of obeying, using sand from the stream bottom for soap to scrub her body. Next she washed her hair, then drew things out by still scrubbing herself long after she was clean. When she was finally done her guard called to the squaws, who had erected the tepee and were stocking it with blankets.

Presently the oldest, a tall, white-haired woman, rushed up with a deerskin dress and moccasins, deposited them on the bank and went back to help the other squaws. Buffalo Woman pointed at the dress and beckoned to Evelyn, raising the stick for emphasis. Evelyn sensibly heeded, but unhurriedly splashed to the bank. There was no towel of any sort and she was forced to stand there, dripping wet, on display until the sun had dried her body. Thankfully, no one in the village appeared to notice her.

The doeskin dress, decorated with beads and dyed porcupine quills, was snug and struck her about the knees. The similarly decorated moccasins were a better fit. Head held high, Evelyn was marched ahead of Buffalo Woman to the tepee. While they waited before the entrance flap for the bustling squaws to finish inside, Evelyn surveyed the completed structure.

It resembled a tilted cone, with the smoke vent not at the very top but along the tepee's long side. The outer covering did not quite reach the ground, leaving a space about two inches high all the way around, and Evelyn wondered whether that was by design, or if the covering merely wasn't long enough.

The three squaws emerged and Buffalo Woman snapped an order to the older, white-haired squaw who meekly nodded and rushed off. Impelled forward by a strong shove, Evelyn entered the lodge and stood looking about at its interior. While a bare area was left for the fireplace, the rest of the ground was covered with buffalo

146

robes and rugs and blankets of various colours and patterns placed over the turned up edges of the inner lining to seal out any drafts. Evelyn thought it would be hot, but it was surprisingly pleasant inside. Then she realised that the airspace between the liner and the outer covering provided insulation.

"Sit," Buffalo Woman barked, pointing to a buffalo robe on the far side of the lodge.

Anxious to avoid being helped along by another jarring shove, Evelyn quickly strode to the spot and sat. Immediately she wished to change places. Though comfortable the buffalo robe had a pungent musky odour that was as rank as the horse blankets she had slept in for the last few nights. Buffalo Woman ponderously sank down behind her and set about laboriously combing Evelyn's damp hair with a sharp-pointed shell, relishing her distressed gasps whenever its teeth caught in a stubborn tangle.

During the irksome process (which Evelyn was certain would leave her bald) the older squaw returned with an armload of sticks, built a fire in the shallow pit, then left and returned with a stewpot. The savoury aroma of simmering stew reminded Evelyn that she had eaten nothing but dry, tough jerky (and only enough to keep her alive) since her capture — and she was famished! She unsuccessfully tried to divert her mind and grumbling stomach by watching the air current above the hanging liner mingle with the hot air from the fire and push the smoke outside through the high, tilted opening. Finally her trial was over, long blonde hair combed to a glossy, waxy smoothness, Evelyn was free to focus her sole attention on the stewpot.

Rising, Buffalo Woman lumbered to the fire, ladled a heaping bowl of the thick porridge, then, to Evelyn's vast disappointment, retired to a place near the entrance and squatted there, dipping into the substance with her fingers. Evelyn waited expectantly while the older squaw filled another bowl,

148

only to again be disappointed as the woman sat back from the fire and began eating, also with her fingers.

Seeing that she was being ignored, Evelyn had no intention of sitting and starving meekly. She determinedly started to stand and go serve herself. "Sit," Buffalo Woman growled, spitting bits of food from her half-full mouth. Evelyn only glared back at her and stood. Buffalo Woman angrily rattled off orders to the older squaw while emphatically gesturing for Evelyn to sit.

The other woman begrudgingly set down her bowl and began filling another. Evelyn slowly sank back down and watched as, with a sullen face, the squaw brought the wooden bowl to her. Refraining herself from snatching it, Evelyn accepted the bowl and then stared at the contents helplessly, realising there were no utensils.

"Fingers were used before forks," the old squaw said in perfect English.

Evelyn's eyes instantly snapped up and stared directly into the woman's face for the first time. The watery blue eyes and softer, wrinkled, sun-darkened features told that she was indeed a white woman. Evelyn gasped in surprise and started to speak.

"No talk," Buffalo Woman bellowed. "Sarah, go!"

The old woman flashed a mocking smile then turned away, giggling, and returned to the fire. Without another glance at Evelyn, she sat and resumed her interrupted meal. Buffalo Woman grunted and greedily continued her own meal.

Hungry as she was Evelyn hesitated, her mind again upon her fate. Was she intended as a bride for Stone Eagle, or was she destined to spend her life as a servant, like old Sarah? Slowly her stomach reclaimed her thoughts and, emulating the squaws, she dipped her fingers into the warm porridge.

It was pulpy, almost tasteless, mixed with wild greens and thick with bits of meat, both of which she was unfamiliar. Without wanting to do so she recalled stories concerning Indian culinary habits. While said to eat horse, they supposedly favoured mule even more — but the most delectable of all was dog.

Too starved to care, Evelyn wasn't about to enquire. It was eat this or nothing, as her guards certainly were not about to change their food tastes to suit her. Evelyn ate heartily, and was relieved to find that the food did not turn her stomach. Feeling better with each mouthful, she began scheming of ways to escape. Perhaps old Sarah might be enlisted to help her; she would broach the subject when the time was right. Meanwhile she must husband her strength and wait until night. Encouraged, Evelyn ate leisurely and pretended to be totally absorbed in her messy meal.

★ ★ ★

Travis and the Wallers crossed the Rio Grande in the late afternoon and were doggedly following the Comanches' trail toward the mountains when the air abruptly grew cool and an ominous stillness settled over the land. An urgent shout from Andy, lagging in the rear, caused Travis and Lucas to swivel in their saddles and the sight that greeted them left both momentarily mute.

The horizon had vanished, obscured by a dark, rapidly moving, prairie-wide cloud. At first glance it looked like rain — except there previously hadn't been a cloud in the sky.

"Dust storm," Lucas announced grimly, eyeing the approaching cloud.

"We best ride for them mountains," Andy said, bringing his mount up to them.

Travis shook his head. "No time. It'll be on top of us in minutes." He pointed toward a small cluster of rocks about a half-mile to their left. "Not much, but that's a damn sight better than nothing."

"This ain't no time to be picky," Andy said and gigged his horse forward.

As Travis and Lucas charged after him a breeze sprang up behind them, followed by an unearthly moaning that set their nerves on edge. The storm was doing its level best to overtake them — and if that happened they would blindly flounder and perish, suffocated by dust.

The moaning grew to a roar as the sky slowly dimmed and the air became thick and dust-laden. Hoping to keep ahead of the fast-closing cyclonic winds, the men desperately whipped their horses onward.

10

TRAVIS and Lucas reached the six rocks with little time to spare. Andy was already dismounted, tying a blanket over his skittish horse's head. The two men bolted from their saddles and followed his example. There was just time to hastily wet bandannas and draw them over the lower halves of their faces before the howling grey cloud slammed into them.

Holding his horse's reins tightly, Travis sank down with his back against one of the rocks, pulled his shirt collar up high and crammed his hat low over his eyes. The horse stamped and pulled at the reins as the storm increased its fury. Travis wound them around his wrist more securely while the horse continued to snort and plunge.

Despite their closeness the men were

unable to see one another through the thickly flying dust that settled on them and sifted down from the sheltering rocks to almost bury them. The men waited patiently but the storm showed no signs of merely passing them by. They could only hug the rocks, shake off the engulfing dust and breathe shallowly, so as not to inhale too much of it and choke to death.

Travis grimly knew that the storm was already hard at work scouring the ground clean of tracks, and the Comanches' trail would soon be completely gone. It meant a setback but not defeat. He would merely begin a different kind of tracking, and the end would still be the same — one way or another he would find Evelyn.

Then he was forcibly dragged from both his thoughts and the rock shelter by his frightened horse. Belly-down, he was towed several yards across the ground before he could gain his knees and rein in the animal. He blindly clawed his way back to the rock, savagely tugging his resisting horse after him. He hunkered there again and the horse finally settled down, put its rump to the wind and dropped its head.

More dust heaped down on Travis as the wind whipped over and past the rock. His mouth tasted gritty and he wanted to sneeze. The world about him was dark grey. He could barely make out the dim outline of his horse as the wild flurries and gusts sought to isolate him.

The vast roar of the wind did not cease as the storm persisted through the rest of the day and into the night. Dunes piled against the rocks, frequently forcing the men to dig themselves out. Sleep was out of the question during the long, endless hours, for to do so was to be buried alive. But sleep was also made impossible by the noise of sand blasting incessantly against the rocks and the wind shrieking horribly, as if frustrated by the protective barrier.

Peering through slitted eyes into the

grey veil of pelting dust at the darkness beyond, Travis mentally summoned Evelyn's lovely, smiling image and closed himself off from all else. He bitterly resented the delay, but the storm would not last for ever. The pursuit would begin again — and soon Evelyn would be in his arms to stay.

★ ★ ★

Having guzzled a jugful of Apache *tulapai*, a potent corn brew, Buffalo Woman was sprawled in a drunken slumber on a robe near the lodge's entrance. Long used to thc woman's heavy snoring old Sarah slept soundly on the other side of the enclosure. Despite her weary state Evelyn was awake, but it was by choice rather than the grating sounds issuing from Buffalo Woman. No longer being observed she was hard at work trying to rid herself of her rawhide bonds. Regretfully, Buffalo Woman had been sober at the time, and Evelyn was secured in knots which only an Indian could have tied.

Evelyn soon despondently realised that the bands about her wrists, arms, legs and ankles were unyielding and she was only harming her soft flesh. She reluctantly gave up and lay letting the various self-inflicted aches to her tall, slender form subside. Her eyes urgently swept the area for something sharp to cut the thongs, but the only knife lay beside Buffalo Woman. The cooking fire still glowed faintly. She considered, then discarded the idea. There was no way to burn off the thongs without serious injury to her wrists.

After a long moment of silent despair Evelyn resigned herself to waking Sarah and begging her help; a refusal would leave her no more frustrated than she was now. As calling from across the tepee was out of the question, she must manoeuvre herself nearer. She began squirming forward on her side, crablike, and quickly found that her task was easier to contemplate than to accomplish. It was tedious torment, made even more difficult by the necessity of keeping her movements as silent as possible. Biting her lower lip to stifle her pained gasps, she forced her protesting body on by wriggling her shoulders and thrusting with her legs.

Evelyn was over halfway to Sarah when Buffalo Woman gave an abrupt snort and stirred. Breathless, wishing herself invisible, Evelyn huddled motionless. The stout woman raised her head as though listening, then rolled over with a heavy grunt, her back to Evelyn, and soon resumed snoring. Relief flooded through Evelyn, but she cautiously delayed until she was certain the squaw was fast asleep before moving a muscle.

Ever so gradually Evelyn drew to within five feet of Sarah and went limp in her bonds, panting from exhaustion. Aware that she might make more of a sound than she intended, she forced herself to wait for her laboured breathing to return

159

to normal. Only then did she dare call to Sarah in a loud whisper. Instantly the older woman turned to her and smiled.

"I been lying here a-listening to you for some time," Sarah announced, her voice above a whisper. "What do you want of me?"

Your help," Evelyn replied, her voice still a whisper. "I do not want to marry Stone Eagle."

"Land o' Goshen," Sarah said, amused. "Where did you get that idea?" She saw Evelyn's bewilderment and scooted nearer. "This place is the Valley of Tears." As Evelyn's blank stare was not the hoped for reaction, she continued. "The Comancheros and Mexican dons come here to trade at the end of the summer raiding season. The Comancheros want livestock and maybe a woman or two. The dons need slaves for their silver mines, and cattle, horses, and women for their *haciendas*. With your looks and blonde hair, you'll fetch a pretty price." She nodded and took pleasure in adding, You surely will, at that."

Evelyn was momentarily speechless, shaking her head disbelievingly. The old woman's wrinkled grin confirmed her words, and Evelyn's surprise became indignation. She held her tongue and coolly regained her composure. "Sarah, please help me escape. You know the country. We could — "

"Nobody ever helped me," the old woman interrupted sharply. "I been here well over thirty years."

"I'm offering to help you now," Evelyn countered.

You're only thinking of yourself. You're one of them high-class ladies. You wouldn't even speak to me on the street if things were different!

Both women froze as Sarah's rising voice caused Buffalo Woman to stir and heavily roll over. They remained still until the woman's snores again filled the lodge. Evelyn started to speak but Sarah shook her head.

"There's no escape. I tried time and

again, till they threatened to hamstring me if I did it one more time. Things is bad enough without being a cripple. And I don't intend to become one because I helped you."

"Just untie me and I'll go alone," Evelyn implored.

"They would still know I helped you." Sarah motioned towards the rear of the tepee. "Now you just get yourself back where you belong and quit vexing me. Buffalo Woman would love nothing better than to beat the both of us till her arm tired." With that she firmly turned away.

Evelyn lingered, staring dejectedly at the old woman's back, then accepted the truth that there was nothing she could say to change Sarah's mind. Broken in spirit, Sarah was resigned to her lot in life. Evelyn gracelessly rolled over and began the long, wearisome crawl back to her place on the buffalo robe.

★ ★ ★

With the coming of dawn the dust storm finally blew itself out and the wind died to a faint breeze. Magnified by the lingering dusty air, the rising sun was a strange pinkish-orange. Figures grey with dust, Travis and the Wallers stiffly stood, tugged down their bandannas and looked about at the dunes heaped against the rocks. After slapping clouds of dust from their clothes with their hats, the men dug out their partly buried gear, then fed and watered the horses before making breakfast.

They ate in relative silence, Travis bolting his food, anxious to get back on the trail. Lucas was cheerful enough, but Andy's deep scowl did not vanish with his second cup of morning coffee. Something was stuck in the big man's craw and Travis had a pretty good idea what it was. He braced himself for trouble and waited.

It came as they were saddling up.

"Well, we done our best," Andy announced. He rammed a knee into his puffed up horse's ribs, violently driving the air from its lungs with a heavy snort, before tightening the cinch. Yes sir, we got nothin' to be ashamed of. Ol' Davy Crockett hisself couldn't done more.

Travis adjusted his mount's bridle and turned to face Andy. You planning on quitting?" he asked mildly.

"What with no trail to follow, we's just a-wastin' our time. Them Comanches is long gone by now."

"You got pressing business elsewhere?"

"Maybe," the big man replied, planting himself belligerently.

Lucas stepped aboard his saddle and, face twisting in irritation, looked down at his brother. You ain't got nowhere useful to go — and you know it."

"Do what you want, Lucas, but I'm a-goin'," Andy said and turned to mount.

"Not on my horse," Travis said, his cold voice cutting like a whip.

Foot in the stirrup, Andy turned his head toward Travis. "I'm fixin' to pay for 'im."

"I told you before, your money's no good. He stays with me."

"Looks like you're takin' Shanks's mare, Andy," Lucas interjected, amused.

"The hell you say." Andy nodded about at the desolate country. "I ain't a-walkin' outta here." He turned back to mount. He was halfway into the saddle when the deadly click of a six-gun's hammer halted him.

You ain't even walking if you try to take that horse," Travis stated, his voice too calm and casual.

Andy glanced around, saw the Colt that had flashed into Travis' right hand and heavily dropped back to the ground. "No man pulls on me," he growled and, anger flaming, took a defiant step toward Travis, who held his ground and calmly shifted the Colt's muzzle to the centre of the big man's chest.

"Now you don't wantta go startin'

no blood-feud, do you, Travis?" Lucas drawled, sharply cocking the hammer of the Henry lying across his saddle bow.

The question went unanswered and a deathly silence hung in the dust-tainted air.

11

WARY as wolves, the men waited for someone to make his play and start the shooting match. Travis coolly weighed his chances and the wisdom of a shoot-out. He was confident of bringing down both men — but was it worth the risk? Then Lucas made the decision for him.

"But if'n you've a mind to take what's yours without gunplay that'd be a different matter . . . "

Wordlessly Travis slowly leathered his Colt and unbuckled his gunbelt. A huge pleased grin spread over Andy's grimy face and he eagerly shucked his gunbelt.

"You do what you think you should," Lucas said matter-of-factly and shoved the Henry back into its saddle holster. "But it's only fair to tell you that ol' Andy ain't never been licked." He

167

watched Travis move forward to meet Andy and, grinning, hooked a leg over the saddle horn and shoved back his hat brim.

With the mindless eagerness of a dog accepting a fight Andy lunged at Travis, arms swinging. Travis ducked a wild left, stepped in and rammed a hard right into the big man's belly that set him back on his heels. Andy's grin turned sour and he used more care as they began to circle, feinting, dodging, weaving, throwing blows that either missed, or did little damage. Then they closed, clenched fists hammering.

Lucas lazily drew the makings from a shirt pocket and built a cigarette while the men fought for a few minutes, kneeing, smashing and gouging. Travis, then Andy, went down but neither stayed on the ground. Scratching a match to flame on his pommel, Lucas smoked and observed the proceedings. It had been a long spell since he'd seen a truly good fight. The only sounds were the combatants' heavy breathing and grunts of acknowledged pain when a fist landed.

Andy abruptly barrelled in and his huge arms started to circle Travis who smashed his kidneys with both fists. Absorbing the punishing blows, the big man grabbed Travis in a bear-hug. The filthy smell of the man was strong in Travis' nostrils as he was raised off his feet and Andy's big knuckles dug into the small of his back.

Lungs bursting, agony racing the length of his spine, Travis desperately slapped his cupped hands sharply against Andy's ears again and again. Howling his hurt, Andy hurled Travis away from him. Arms and legs thrashing, Travis sailed backwards and crashed to the ground. The violent intensity of the fall smashed the wind from his lungs and blurred his vision.

Holding his smarting ears, Andy reeled about drunk with torment. He recovered, lumbered to Travis' stunned form and raised a boot high to stomp on his face. Travis urgently threw his hands up, caught the descending boot and gave a hard wrench. Off balance, Andy went sprawling backwards and slammed heavily to the ground in a huge cloud of dust.

Cigarette ignored, Lucas stared as the men gained their feet and met with a jolting crash. Travis quickly hooked a short, hard blow to Andy's ribs and sent him backstepping. Then he suddenly sprang forward, clouted a vicious fist against Andy's ear, bringing a roar of anguish and frustration, and danced back out of the big man's arm reach. Lucas flipped his cigarette away as its burning tip neared his fingers and shook his head. It sure looked like that, for the first time, his burly brother had met up with a fella who just might be a match for him.

Travis slyly circled Andy around with his back to a rock, then moved in swiftly. He took an overhanded blow on the back just before his shoulder rammed into Andy's midriff and ground hard. The air came rushing out of Andy in huge gasps. The big man clawed for his hair but Travis twisted aside and unleashed a wicked uppercut with all the strength he could muster. Bone crunched on bone as his fist caught Andy squarely under the chin and savagely rapped his shaggy head back against the rock.

Travis wheeled away as Andy, the fight ebbing from him, began to slump down the rock. Fists pumping, he came boring in again, determined to make his victory decisive. Andy feebly tried to cover his body with his leaden arms but Travis abruptly switched his attack to the big man's face. Arms limp at his sides, head snapping back and forth with the smashing blows, Andy slowly continued to slide down the rock. Travis aided his progress by kicking a foot out from under him and Andy slammed down on his haunches, then toppled over sideways.

"Figure you're done?" Lucas enquired, a hint of finality in his casual tone, as he allowed his horse to drift toward the men.

Winded, Travis stepped back from Andy's semi-conscious bulk and turned to look up at Lucas. "As long as he is . . . " he managed between heavy gasps.

"From the looks of 'im you'll git no more argument from Andy," Lucas said, his voice devoid of animosity.

"Then I'll be taking my horse and leaving."

"I'd still like to ride with you, if you've a mind?"

"What about him?" Travis asked, nodding to Andy who was now groaning and stirring.

"He can fend for hisself."

"He's your brother," Travis said with an unconcerned shrug and strode off.

Lucas looked down as Andy clumsily shoved himself to a sitting position and leaned back against the rock. "Well, you finally run up again' somebody you couldn't bully." Andy stared up at him groggily. Lucas gestured after

Travis. "You'd best go make amends with him, 'fore you git left behind."

Andy glared over at Travis, strapping on his gunbelt, then spat some blood and muttered an obscenity. He wiped his mouth with the back of a hand and shifted his sullen gaze back to Lucas.

"Suit yourself," Lucas said easily. "But I'm still bound and determined to fetch back them furs — with or without your help."

Andy made no comment and continued sitting there like a huge poison toad. It was only when Lucas and Travis, leading his spare horse, started away without a backward glance that common sense goaded him to his feet and sent him charging after them, waving and bellowing.

Luckily, they decided to halt and wait for him.

★ ★ ★

Evelyn and the two squaws breakfasted on last night's warmed over porridge while listening to the sounds of much activity coming from both Indian camps. Old Sarah guiltily avoided her questioning eyes and appeared preoccupied in her bland meal, leaving Buffalo Woman's wide smirk to confirm her guess that the Mexican traders had arrived. Evelyn tensed as a rider drew up outside and Stone Eagle's impressive form was seen through the open entrance flap. He barked a command in Comanche and Buffalo Woman popped the last heaping handful of porridge into her mouth, then, cheeks bulging, hurried out to him.

Evelyn again glanced to Sarah, hoping she would translate the rapid, sing-song conversation, but the old woman was now engaged in meticulously licking her messy fingers clean. The conversation ended and Stone Eagle rode off. Buffalo Woman bustled back inside and snapped orders to Sarah in Comanche. Taking an empty bowl, the old white squaw quickly disappeared outside.

You eat plenty fast," Buffalo Woman said, motioning impatiently to Evelyn. "Soon we go."

"Where?" Evelyn enquired suspiciously.

"Eat!" Scowling, arms folded, the heavyset woman stood waiting while Evelyn, her appetite greatly diminished, finished the remnants of her meal.

Presently old Sarah returned with a bowl of water and a handful of red berries. Evelyn gratefully washed her face and hands, then reluctantly sat still while Buffalo Woman neatly combed her slightly dishevelled hair to a golden sheen. The berries were crushed and her lips brightly dyed with the juice. A string of shells and coloured beads was draped about her neck as added decoration, and Buffalo Woman rudely drew her up by one bare arm. Evelyn stood wincing while both women vigorously brushed her deerskin dress clean of dirt and stray food particles, their hands almost bruising her flesh beneath in the process. Buffalo Woman gave an order and old Sarah hastily fetched some lengths of rawhide.

Knowing it would be futile to protest or resist, Evelyn sighed her displeasure and obediently clasped her hands together behind her back. She wriggled her slim shoulders a little but didn't give Buffalo Woman the satisfaction of voicing a complaint as the stout squaw deftly tied her wrists and looped the long thong up her arms, knotting it above her touching elbows. Buffalo Woman stepped back to critically study Evelyn's appearance, then nodded and grunted in satisfaction and motioned her toward the tepee opening.

"Pretty as a picture," old Sarah cackled. "You're gonna make some don awful happy — and Stone Eagle awful rich!"

"Sarah, shut mouth!" Buffalo Woman warned, seeing Evelyn blanch and take a step backward as she was again reminded of her fate. She seized Evelyn's shoulder and thrust her forward.

Evelyn blinked at the early morning

176

sunlight striking her eyes as Buffalo Woman pushed her outside the tepee and followed with Sarah, who still carried other rawhide strips. Stiff-legged, she was escorted away between the two squaws.

Most of the village had emptied and the few Indians remaining were too busy gathering articles for barter to spare more than a glance at Evelyn and the women. As they passed along a row of tepees, Evelyn soon noticed that all of the openings faced east toward the rising sun. She managed a look across the stream and saw that the Apache wicki-ups were similarly arranged. The fact had escaped her yesterday, as she had been too distracted by the curious and hostile faces watching her arrival. She guessed that it must be a religious practice followed by all of the Indian tribes. The distant commotion grew louder as they neared the end of the village and Evelyn grew cold with apprehension at the thought of what awaited her.

On rounding the last tepee they looked out on a festive scene that, at a distance, deceptively resembled a county fair and was being played out on both sides of the stream. Gaily-coloured silken tents were pitched in shady glades with dark carriages and Mexican *carretas*, tall carts with two huge wooden wheels, clustered nearby. Gaudy *vaqueros* in high peaked, floppy brimmed hats, large silver spurs jingling, swaggered about conducting trade while elegantly dressed dons sat on camp chairs and aloofly looked on. White-clad servants came in and out of the tents bearing silver trays laden with refreshments for their individual masters.

Pausing, Evelyn stared past the group toward a string of horsemen, carriages and oxen-drawn *carretas* emerging into the valley from the mouth of the canyon. They were met by mounted Apache and Comanche braves who eagerly competed in trying to steer the newcomers to their individual market places. Buffalo Woman's irritable shove snapped Evelyn's head back on her shoulders and sent her stumbling forward.

As she drew nearer the trading area Evelyn was bewildered by the babel of languages spoken. At first glance the trade appeared innocent enough. The Mexicans were offering bolts of bright cloth, leatherware and garments and old-fashioned muzzle-loading rifles for horses, gold objects and colourful Indian blankets. Then there was a break in the group gathered around one of the makeshift corrals and she saw it held captive men instead of livestock. Though she had already been told of the slave labour used in the Mexican silver mines the sight of the wretched, half-naked Anglos, Indians and even Mexicans still startled Evelyn as the full awareness of her own predicament crashed in on her. Soon she would be standing inside a corral with men's hungry eyes upon her. The thought filled her with abhorrence and made her want to turn and run.

Suddenly Stone Eagle, tall war bonnet fluttering, came pounding toward them and jerked his pony to a halt, barring the way. As his impersonal eyes roamed over her appraisingly Evelyn was uncomfortably conscious of the snugly moulding dress emphasising her splendid figure. The suggestion of a smile crossed his face and he grunted his approval. After a brief exchange of words with Buffalo Woman in their own language, he wheeled his pony and trotted away.

You come," the stout squaw said, taking Evelyn by a shoulder and firmly turning her around.

Evelyn threw a confused glance to Sarah but was shoved forward before she could voice a question. For a foolish moment her spirits rose as they marched back toward the village. Perhaps she was not to be sold after all? Did that mean the chief had decided to keep her for himself? The thought was not comforting, but it meant she would remain in the village — and that would give Travis more time to find the valley. She started to let her thoughts dwell on Travis but the pleasant distraction did not last long. Buffalo Woman's strong fingers burrowed into her upper arm and turned her away from the village toward a large solitary tree beside the stream.

When they reached the tree Evelyn was shoved down in the shade with her back against its trunk. Taking a long thong from Sarah, Buffalo Woman issued a gruff order in Comanche and began to tether Evelyn to the tree by her bound wrists. Evelyn winced as old Sarah used the remaining rawhide on her legs and seemed to derive a strange pleasure from drawing the loops so tight that her knee and ankle bones rubbed together painfully. But she quickly understood that the old woman's motivation had been fear as she watched Sarah fidget nervously while Buffalo Woman carefully inspected the knots she had tied. The tension faded from Sarah's wrinkled face as Buffalo Woman nodded and moved away.

"Sarah, what does this mean?" Evelyn asked in a low tone, leaning away from the trunk and looking up at her.

The old woman's eyes cautiously darted to Buffalo Woman, who was selecting a cudgel from one of the dead limbs on the bank, then back to Evelyn. "Just be patient, dearie, your time's a-coming." She smiled and gestured toward the market area. "Stone Eagle is waiting for some special folks to arrive. Real rich ones who'll pay through the nose to own a white gal with blonde hair and blue eyes."

Buffalo Woman returned with her stout stick, ordered Sarah to the other side of the tree to watch the Apache side of the stream and took up a position near Evelyn, ready to chase away any intruders from the Comanche trading area.

Evelyn once again felt her hopes fading as she uneasily wondered how long her reprieve would last. By turning her head from side to side she was able to see most of the market places scattered on either side of the stream, and a perverse fascination compelled her to watch the hectic activities. Still the sights and sounds could not divert her from her own morbid thoughts for long and she tensed as every new arrival entered the valley. Waiting was unbearable — but she knew the end would be far worse.

12

FOR well over an hour now Travis and the Wallers had been manoeuvering through the tortuous folds of the canyon. Each man kept his own silence, and only the occasional chink of a shod hoof striking the surface of a rock broke the monotonous echo of jingling bits and creaking leather. Though the chance of ambush was slight the three men were nevertheless alert to the possibility, and their eyes suspiciously ranged the towering walls.

Finally they were free of the canyon and looking out at a broad, grass-sprinkled valley. The storm had stirred up the ground there too and wiped out any obvious trail the Comanches might have left. Without pausing for useless discussion Travis booted his mount forward and cantered straight out across the valley. Lucas and Andy silently followed, spreading wide to either side of Travis and studying the ground as they rode.

Midway inside the valley the men dismounted to stretch their legs and slowly lead their tired horses. The late morning sun was warm on their backs as the men trudged along, experienced eyes sharply scowering the ground before them. Shirt sticky and uncomfortable, Andy mopped his face with a bandanna and grumbled incoherent curses about everything in general.

"Best not dally long in this too-open valley," Lucas called ahead to Travis. "We make awful fine targets." His head swivelled from side to side, studying the rocky boundaries around them.

"Damn wise words, Lucas," Andy eagerly seconded.

Travis made no acknowledgement; even though he shared the men's uneasiness he was determined to search every inch of the valley, if necessary, until he found the Comanches' trail. Lucas fell silent and continued dividing his attention between the ground and the mountains while Andy resumed berating one and all. They walked on for a few dozen yards and then Travis detected something.

Kneeling, Travis stared at a small patch of trampled grass. His fingers explored and found the indentations made by a horseshoe. Most likely one of the horses taken from the Waller brothers hunting party. He called the men over and they gathered around him and studied his find.

"Looks to be them all right," Lucas agreed. He looked toward the far end of the valley. "But I sure don't see no passage ahead."

"They just sprouted wings and flew right over that there mesa," Andy said caustically, to no one's amusement but his own.

"There's a way out," Travis said flatly. He got a foot in the stirrup and swung a leg over the saddle. "And we'll find it." He started off at a trot, leaving the two men to mount and trail after him.

They pushed on to the end of the valley, finding an occasional track of a shod horse as they went. The signs of many scrambling horses were plainly seen leading up a sharply twisting slope of an arroyo. The men eyed the trail of sorts dubiously, not relishing the hard climb.

"So that's how they done it," Lucas remarked.

"Aw, there's gotta be an easy way," Andy said, looking about the base.

"If there is, don't you think they'd have took it?" Lucas said disgustedly.

"Wouldn't hurt nothin' to poke around some, Andy insisted.

"We don't have time to waste," Travis said firmly and started his mount up the steep slope.

"C'mon, Andy," Lucas said almost cheerfully. "Anythin' an Injun can do so can we."

Andy sat scowling as he watched

Lucas scramble up after Travis. He shook his head and heaved a heavy sigh of resignation. "Hoss, you fall on me," he growled, "and I'll shoot you right atwixt the eyes." He put his spurs to the animal and sent it charging up after the others.

It was a hard struggle, but finally the three men clambered up over the top of the crest and out on a wide mesa. They exchanged relieved glances and wordlessly proceeded on, letting their heaving horses walk slowly until they had recovered from the ordeal.

★ ★ ★

The Valley of Tears was aptly named. Throughout the long morning Evelyn watched the misery taking place around her. Batches of haggard men and sobbing women were spiritedly traded to stately dons and rough, drink-sodden Comancheros, then loaded into the giant basket bodies of *carretas* and, enormous, ungreased wheels screeching in torment with every revolution, taken off to their various unpleasant fates. Evelyn could not keep from wondering how long it would be until she too shared a *carreta* with other unfortunates, and found it becoming increasingly difficult to maintain her confidence that she would be rescued in time.

While mules, cattle and mustangs were disposed of in lots, thoroughbreds, still bearing brands of Texas ranches from which they had been stolen, were traded individually, and Evelyn found those auctions merciful distractions. But her depression soon returned with the auction of a variety of plundered articles, ranging from hand-tooled saddles, some glittering with silver ornaments, to rocking chairs and baby cradles, and she vainly tried not to speculate on what tragedies had befallen their previous owners.

Buffalo Woman maintained her vigil, brandishing her club and shrieking dire threats whenever Indian, Mexican or

Comanchero curiously passed too close to Evelyn's tree while wandering back and forth across the stream from the Apache and Comanche trading areas. Intent on keeping the shaky peace and engaging in profitable commerce none created an incident by challenging her authority, though more than a few flung curses at her. Occasionally Evelyn caught sight of Stone Eagle's proud figure riding through the colourful, jostling crowd as he oversaw the auctions, and she was thankful that he was preoccupied with matters other than her own sale.

At noon there came a lull in the auctions, and a general relaxed rowdiness settled over the area. The dons aloofly retired to the comfort of their tents and the others ate, drank and gambled in various groups. Old Sarah fetched food and drink while Buffalo Woman kept watchful guard over Evelyn. It was needless for the men were engrossed in games of dice or cards, but the act fed the stout woman's need of self-importance.

After the squaws had eaten Sarah hand fed Evelyn bits of meat from a bowl, washed down by a gourd of water from the stream. The unsettling scenes she'd witnessed had curbed her appetite, but Evelyn ate and used the opportunity to question Sarah.

"Mexicans like their *siesta*," the old woman said brightly, "so nothing's going to happen until the middle of the afternoon, when things get cooler." She offered a piece of meat to Evelyn, then shrugged and popped it into her own mouth when the captive shook her head.

"Does Stone Eagle still plan to sell me today?" Evelyn asked, leaning forward as far as the rawhide tethering her wrists to the tree would allow.

Sarah nodded, put another bit of meat into her mouth, and said as she chewed, "He's waiting on Ramon Segara. A scout brought word his waggons are only a few miles away."

"Is he a wealthy Spanish don?"

Old Sarah cackled so hard she almost choked on her food. "Lands, no. He's the biggest and most feared bandit in all of Northern Mexico — even the dons want no truck with him." She ran her eyes over Evelyn's face and figure. "Don't be surprised if he don't up and take you for his new little *muchacha* . . . least ways till he tires of you and gives you to his men." She saw Evelyn's uneasiness and broke into another round of laughter.

Evelyn felt a rising anger and tugged at her bindings. "You enjoy taunting me — why?" she demanded, staring hotly into the old woman's eyes.

Surprised by Evelyn's intensity Sarah abruptly fell silent. Frowning curiously, she sat back, cocked her head and moved her lips wordlessly, as if struggling to arrange her thoughts coherently. Finally she said haltingly, "For years and years I seen white women come and go. If I was to bother my head about them I'd go right crazy." She shrugged and looked away from Evelyn's withering gaze. "But sometimes I can't help myself and I get to thinking . . . and I envy them."

"Envy?" Evelyn repeated in dismay.

Sarah turned back, her withered face touched by sadness, and nodded. "Maybe just one of them found a better life than this," she motioned about her, "and a man to love her — even if it's only for a little while. That's something I never had — and now I never will." She quickly rose with the dish and gourd and hurried away.

Evelyn turned but Sarah had already vanished and the trunk obscured her vision. She sadly thought about the old woman's long years as an outcast with a hostile people, and then her thoughts slowly turned inward. But she still had hope. The Latin custom of taking an afternoon nap after eating gave her a reprieve of several hours — and anything might happen during that time.

★ ★ ★

The exposed mesa top offered no protection as the scorching early afternoon sun lay its bright heat upon the land. Travis and the Waller boys felt the hot earth burning right up through the soles of their boots as they walked on steadily but slowly, leading their wheezing horses and taking care to hoard their strength. No one talked; it was too much of a bother, and there was nothing useful to say.

Borrowing an old Indian trick to further conserve water, each man held a pebble in his mouth, which helped to keep his mouth and throat from going dry. Still, the measure would only work for a time, and then they would have to drink. All knew of cases where some overzealous fool had died of dehydration with water still in his canteen.

The trail continued across the broad mesa, whose sheer sides discouraged any hope of leaving its top and hunting for further tracks along its base. All the men could do was follow the trail to its end, or else backtrack to the valley they had left and search for another way out. Not only would that be a waste of time, they might not even pick up the trail again. Concentrating on placing one foot ahead of the other and keeping their forward motion going, the men plodded on across the broiling mesa.

13

FINALLY the deep scars the heavily loaded pack horses' iron shoes had cut into the rocky surface veered off and ended at the mesa's edge. The three men stood looking at a meagre trail that angled down to a small, grassy valley and then tensed expectantly at the sight of three mule-drawn waggons lumbering toward a tall granite mountain. Over twenty well armed outriders accompanied the waggons, whose tattered canvas tops mostly concealed their contents.

"Must be haulin' somethin' mighty valuable," Andy speculated.

"Comancheros on their way to trade," Lucas said flatly.

"If this is the Valley of Tears," Travis asked, surveying the area, "then where are the Comanches?"

"This don't appear to be it exactly,"

Lucas answered. "But if'n we just follow that bunch we'll find it sure."

They continued watching in silence, and presently the waggons and riders entered a passage that was not visible from the mesa top. The three exchanged quick looks.

"What'd I tell you?" Lucas said smugly. "Now my guess is that the Valley of Tears lies right on the other side of that mountain."

"Saying it is," Travis agreed, watching the steeple-hatted Mexican riders trailing the last waggon into the pass, "how do we get in there?"

"It ain't exactly open to the public," Lucas said. He rubbed his dark stubbled cheek thoughtfully. "Even though we's a disreputable lookin' lot, they got secret signs and words we don't know." He shook his head. "Best to wait till dark and slip in there on foot."

"On foot!" Andy snorted. "We can't tote all them furs out on our backs."

"There'll be plenty of horses to steal

197

when the time comes."

"But Evelyn could have been sold by then," Travis objected.

"Then you'll see her leavin' and won't have to set foot in there."

"And if she's already been sold and taken away I won't know for hours."

Lucas made a sweeping gesture. "You're free to follow any tracks leading away from here, or ride straight in there and git yourself kilt or sold to some Sonora mine-ownin' don. But our mama," he indicated himself and Andy, "didn't raise no fool jackasses."

"She sure enough didn't," Andy seconded emphatically.

Travis fretted impotently, then reluctantly bridled his impatience and surrendered to logic. "All right," he said calmly. "But as soon as that group is lost from sight we're getting down from here and across that valley to a spot where we can watch the pass close up."

"No argument," Lucas said amiably. "Now that we's all of one mind,"

Andy said, 'supposin' we git back some and stop sky-linin' this mesa for all to see." He turned and led the way back to the waiting horses.

★ ★ ★

Evelyn was jarred from her fitful sleep by yells, gunshots and thundering hoofs and waggons. For a wild moment she thought they were being attacked and rescue was finally at hand. Unfortunately that hope was short-lived.

"Here comes Ramon Segara," old Sarah called excitedly, staring toward the pass, her voice almost lost in the tumult.

Evelyn caught her breath sharply, every fibre of her body, every nerve end taut, and peered past the moving bodies of the welcoming throng. Turning her head from side to side and arching her slender neck, she stared so hard her eyes ached. Then the men had cleared away and she was able to see a large group of horsemen, pistols and rifles firing into the air, galloping ahead of three covered waggons that were not the *carretas* she had become used to seeing. Stone Eagle and several braves rode out to meet the approaching caravan. The Apache leader and some of his whooping warriors came splashing across the stream and galloped to join the group.

"Soon you'll have admirers swarming around you like bees to honey," Sarah said, her wrinkled face glowing. "The bidding is going to be right lively, to say the least." She lapsed into her irritating cackle.

Evelyn was too intent on trying to catch a glimpse of the notorious Ramon Segara to pay much attention to Sarah's taunting prediction. Besides, screaming her frustration would be a futile waste of emotion that would only further encourage the old woman. The horsemen rode out of her limited line of vision and she was unsuccessful in sighting the Mexican bandit. Evelyn leaned back against the tree and waited, her spirit dejected by the knowledge that it would not be long before her own auction was at hand.

Within an hour Evelyn saw Stone Eagle riding toward her in the company of four men. Three were finely dressed dons on sleek thoroughbreds while the fourth was garishly dressed and rode a wiry mustang. Evelyn had no doubt that he must be Ramon Segara. The men pulled up a short distance before her and dismounted. Stone Eagle led the four to Evelyn, proudly indicated her with a grand gesture, then stepped aside and stood, arms folded across his chest, while the men crowded around her. Instead of cowering Evelyn held herself as erect as her bonds permitted and stared up boldly at the men.

The dons ranged from early middle-age to a stately white-haired man. Their features were pure Spanish and their linen shirts and velvet suits spotless. In contrast the fourth man was tall, muscular and had the hard, swarthy features so identified with *peons* of mixed blood. He wore tight-fitting, gaudy trousers ornamented with silver from boot to thigh, a short leather jacket over an embroidered shirt and a steeple-crowned hat. But what all four men did have in common was an eager stare as their burning, black eyes mentally undressed her.

Evelyn was painfully aware of her firm bosom straining against her snug dress and relaxed her rigid position, diminishing the emphasis somewhat. Still she felt the men's meticulous eyes crawling like invisible insects over the entire length of her tall, superb form. The fourth man grinned and stepped closer. For an awful moment Evelyn feared that he would lean down and touch her. Then one of the dons spoke questioningly to Stone Eagle in Spanish and the fourth man turned away as the Indian replied. Evelyn drew a calming breath as the men moved to Stone Eagle and began a discussion.

The men spoke in rapid Spanish, with a few words of Comanche interjected from time to time. The talk began good-naturedly but soon became loud and animated, except for Stone Eagle and the white-haired don. It was not necessary for Evelyn to speak Spanish to know that the Comanche chief had demanded a high price for her and was firmly determined to have it. He was impervious to the Mexicans' threats and cajolings as the men stood there discussing her as if she were a prized thoroughbred.

Gesturing and shaking his head vehemently, one don turned, stalked to his horse and then hesitated, evidently hoping to be called back after his grand display of Latin temper. He wasn't. Ramming a boot into a flaring leather covered stirrup, he hauled himself aboard his fancy silver saddle and galloped away. A few minutes later the second don made a huffy departure and the bidding was narrowed to the elderly don and Ramon Segara.

Silently praying that the remaining men would also refuse to meet Stone

Eagle's demand, Evelyn tensely watched as the negotiations resumed. Finally the bandit took the white-haired don aside and talked earnestly, persuasively. The older man paled and stiffened as though insulted, then blustered indignantly while the bandit merely smiled nastily. Defeated but determined to save face, he whirled on a heel and strode away with all the dignity he could muster. Segara returned to Stone Eagle and both were oblivious to the don's scornful eyes as he mounted and aloofly rode off.

Evelyn's misgivings heightened as the transaction was swiftly concluded to the men's mutual satisfaction. Thankfully Ramon Segara did not remain to gloat over his prize. Stone Eagle called brisk orders to Buffalo Woman, then he and the bandit mounted and rode across the stream to the Apache encampment.

Buffalo Woman's lofty command sent Sarah scurrying to Evelyn. As the old woman tugged at the stubborn knots she had previously tied, she remarked, "Stone Eagle made himself a right smart deal — six hundred repeating rifles." She paused and looked at Evelyn's numbed face. "You can be real proud that Ramon Segara values your company that highly." Receiving no response, she disappointedly returned to her task and was urged along by Buffalo Woman's impatient bellow.

A flurry of disjointed thoughts and emotions ran rampant through Evelyn's mind as she vainly fought against the acceptance of her new status. Reality finally took root and she bit her lower lip and fought to hold back tears. She was now a slave: the property of a bandit who would do with her as he pleased.

Evelyn was so absorbed that she was not aware she had been freed from the tree until old Sarah struggled to raise her up by her bound arms. Her uncoordinated legs gave way and she toppled over on her side, dragging the squealing woman down on top of her. Muttering in annoyance, Buffalo

Woman rushed up, quickly untangled the two by shoving Sarah aside, then yanked Evelyn to her unstable feet and thrust her back against the tree, where she was allowed to stand until her legs could support her. Taking the end of the long tether still attached to Evelyn's tied wrists, Buffalo Woman drew her from the tree and pushed her stumblingly forward. Old Sarah scooped up the other lengths of rawhide and sidled after them.

Still immersed in thoughts about her gloomy prospects, Evelyn was almost oblivious to the long walk back through the village, past her former lodgings, and on to a huge tepee, its base eighteen feet across, that had been placed thirty yards above the stream. Several of Ramon Segara's cruel-looking men were taking their time unloading one of the three unhitched waggons grouped about, the mules and horses tied Army fashion to a picket rope a short distance away. Some men were opening cases of new, gleaming repeating rifles and cartridges while others squatted with greasy cards around a small pile of gold and silver coins. All paused to watch with covetous gleams as the squaws passed with their blonde captive. Many rowdy comments were made in Spanish, which Evelyn was certain were vulgar.

On entering the lodge Evelyn was grateful to find no one else there. She was led to a far back side and shoved down on a thick pallet of blankets and skins, then sat unresisting while Sarah retied her legs and ankles and Buffalo Woman looped the long thong around her waist and up her body, pinning her arms against her back, and knotted it at her shoulders. Buffalo Woman grunted to Sarah and started away. The old woman lingered on the pretext of checking the knots she'd tied.

"You just be nice to Ramon Segara and you'll make out right well." She nodded toward the open entrance. "None of them outside will pester you. They know Segara will skin 'em

alive and hang their hides up to dry."
Buffalo Woman called sharply from
outside. Sarah lurched to her feet, gave
a faint parting smile and hurried out,
closing a hide flap over the entrance.

Evelyn glanced about at her bare
surroundings, illuminated by the sunlight
streaming down through the tilted
smoke hole, and tensed at the sound
of men moving about near the tepee.
But it soon became evident that Sarah
had been right: no one was willing
to risk the bandit leader's wrath by
looking in on her. As there was nothing
to do but await Ramon Segara's arrival,
Evelyn awkwardly lay down and strove
to compose her thoughts.

Judging by what she had seen, the
bandit apparently did not intend to
leave the valley any time soon. That
was fine with her, as it would still
give Travis an opportunity to find her.
Hopes nurtured, she relaxed as best
she could and tried to enjoy the first
privacy of sorts that she'd had since her
capture.

★ ★ ★

Ensconced in a nest of rocks overlooking the entrance to the pass, Travis and the Wallers found little to occupy their time until nightfall. Plans made, weapons checked and re-checked, the men took turns dozing only to be awakened by the horrible, deafening screech of *carreta* wheels echoing through the canyon as a trader left the Valley of Tears. Each time Travis anxiously studied the huge carts as they lumbered by and was relieved not to see Evelyn amongst the human cargo. But there was still the nagging fear that she had been sold and transported from the valley earlier.

He begrudged the forced inactivity now that his goal was, hopefully, so near at hand. It gave him time for other thoughts — and one in particular was unsettling. Would he rescue Evelyn and then lose her because of the many hardships she had suffered? He could not blame her if she decided to return to New Orleans. She would want him to accompany her, but ranching was his way of life and he wouldn't be happy in a big city. Well, it was something that would only be truly settled when he had Evelyn back.

Reminding himself to take things one step at a time, Travis restlessly watched the sun slowly continue its path westward.

14

COARSE wool grating her cheek, Evelyn lay drowsing on a colourful blanket. Though her tall body complained at remaining immobile so long, she wasted none of her strength in useless struggle against her rawhide bonds. The voices in Spanish and the *chink* of the men's large-rowelled charro spurs outside the tepee made clear that escape was impossible.

The fading sunlight filtering through the smoke hole told that many hours had passed since the squaws had left her here, after her humiliating sale to the bandit leader for six hundred repeating rifles. Evelyn was still incensed at the thought of being anyone's chattel. She stiffened as voices were raised in greeting to an approaching rider. The horse halted nearby, then heavy, jingling footsteps purposefully approached the lodge.

Shaking her hair from her face, Evelyn craned her neck as the hide flap was flung aside and Ramon Segara followed the sunlight into the lodge. She rolled onto her side as he strode to her and stood smiling. His eyes crawled the full length of her slender form and finally settled on her pale, upturned face.

You make a fetching squaw, *gringa*," he announced, his heavily-accented voice tinged with mockery. "Perhaps I will keep you in that dress when we return to my mountain *casar*?"

Exquisite features set in a scowl of barely contained rage, Evelyn boiled inwardly but wisely held her tongue. Her cool silence only amused him. She winced as his strong hands effortlessly raised her rigid body to a sitting position, then drew her knees up before her defensively as he sank down beside her.

"You should consider yourself most fortunate to be the woman of such an important man. Soon I shall also become a great man in your own country." Evelyn's dubious expression prompted him to elaborate.

"With the guns and whisky I have brought I will unite both the Comanches and Apaches, and then sweep across the Rio Bravo into Texas. The *gringos* have been weakened by years of civil war, and there is still much unrest. They cannot withstand the savagery of my combined forces. And when my countrymen have seen my success they will join me by the thousands. I will take back all of the lands the gringos have stolen from Mexico."

"You will fail," Evelyn said incredulously.

Segara grinned widely and shook his head. "I always get what I want. Don Francisco was prepared to outbid me for you, but I took him aside and vowed to burn his *hacienda* to the ground with him and his family inside. He knows I am a man of my word, and so he made no further bids." He gave a broad shrug. "Don Francisco is an old man and would have been a very bad lover. You would not have been happy with him." Evelyn again tensed as his muscular arm snaked around her shoulders. "Now you may show me your gratitude."

Evelyn made no reply and regarded him with icy disdain. His hand moved up to her hair, forcing her head back so savagely she feared her neck would snap, and his mouth fastened on hers in a lusting hunger, bruising her soft lips against her teeth. Evelyn offered no resistance and kept her lips carefully unresponsive.

For a time Segara continued mauling her mouth demandingly and then sat back irritably. "You *gringas* are all like ice," he declared as Evelyn wiped her mouth on a shoulder of her dress and eyed him contemptuously. "But in time you will learn to behave like a real woman." Defiance flashed in Evelyn's eyes but she did not break her austere silence.

"*Jefe*," called a voice from outside. Segara answered and the man leaned inside the opening. There was a rapid exchange in Spanish, which Evelyn did not understand, then the man withdrew.

"I must meet with Alchisay and Stone Eagle," Segara informed Evelyn as he stood. "When my business is done I shall enjoy taming you, my cold one." His smile was as unpleasant as his meaning.

Evelyn retained her haughty veneer until Segara left, drawing the flap closed and plunging the lodge into semidarkness, before surrendering to concern. Once she was taken to the bandit's mountain hideout, how would Travis ever find her?

★ ★ ★

The two Indians guarding the canyon fell silently beneath Lucas and Andy's knives, and Travis and the men stood surveying the twin camps strung out on

215

either side of the stream.

"They's a whole heap of 'Paches here, too," Andy said, his eyes sweeping the temporary wicki-ups on the far bank.

"Don't pay them no attention at all," Lucas said. "What we want is on the Comanche side."

"And let's get at it," Travis said, leading the way toward the tepees which glowed like Japanese lanterns, their tops, above the inner-liners, shining brighter than their ghostly bases.

Keeping to the tall grass, the men slowly and cautiously made their way to the outskirts of the Comanche village and then split up. Travis figured it would be the last he saw of the Wallers, as they would probably grab their furs and scoot. Skirting the rear of the tepees, whose inner liners made the occupants invisible, as well as prevented them from seeing shadows cast on the outside walls, Travis moved to the far side of the village. He spotted a lodge set a short distance away from the others and, guessing that any captive

216

would be kept separated from the village, stole toward it.

Travis had almost reached the tepee when a woman emerged and walked toward the stream. Knife ready, he halted in a crouch and stared after her. The woman was white, her hair pale in the moonlight, and wore a torn dress. Why would a captive be given free run of the camp — unless, maybe, she was wed to a Comanche? Travis crept forward on soundless feet.

The woman reached the bank and stood staring down at her reflection in the moonlit water. For a fleeting moment Travis had the wild hope that the tall, slender woman might somehow be Evelyn. But as he silently drew nearer that hope vanished. Sensing his presence, the woman turned. He lunged and bore her to the ground, a hand clamping over her mouth and shutting off her cry.

"I don't aim to hurt you," he whispered, his mouth close to her ear, "but don't make an outcry."

217

He held the knife before her face and her struggles immediately stilled. Keeping his hand over her mouth, he continued. "A lone white woman — blonde, beautiful — was brought here yesterday by a raiding party from Texas. Evelyn Carlisle. New Orleans."

Recognition slowly came over Sarah's wrinkled face and she nodded and mumbled unintelligibly. Travis' hand loosened over her mouth, but the blade still hovered threateningly. She licked her lips and spoke low. "In all my time with the Comanches nobody ever had the grit to come steal his woman back. If'n she's the one I think, Ramon Segara has bought her for his own."

Travis felt his muscles go taut at the mention of the bandit. "Are they still here?" he asked grimly. The old woman hesitated, fear and suspicion evident in her face and watery eyes. Travis was tempted to scare the answer out of her with the knife, then thought better and lowered it. "I promise no one will know you told me," he said earnestly. "Now where do I find Evelyn?"

Sarah's expressive face mirrored the inner conflict warring inside her. Finally, she said, "Down yonder is a big lodge. She's tied in there. You'll hafta sneak past the men guarding her."

Travis stood, gently drawing Sarah up with his free hand and staring into her eyes. "Help me, and I'll take you out of here with Evelyn." Instead of bringing hope, his well-intended words set off a violent reaction.

"Nobody must ever see me," Sarah shrieked, yanking her arm free and wildly shaking her head. "I can't never go back. I'd die first!" With startling agility for her age, she avoided Travis' reaching hand and whirled and dashed back toward the lodge, babbling in English and Comanche.

Shocked, Travis stared after the fleeing woman and desperately drew back his knife arm for a throw. Compassion and repugnance at killing an old woman combined to stay his hand. Then, remembering that a knife gave one a choice of point or hilt, he shifted his grip for a less deadly throw.

But before the knife could leave his hand Sarah, framed in the tepee entrance, gave an abrupt jerk and her words became a bubbling cry. One hand clutched the hide flap while the other reached back to flutteringly claw at a knife hilt protruding beneath her left shoulder blade. Then her arched body collapsed, spasmed, and was unnaturally still.

A shape detached itself from the shadows and strode into the moonlight. "Gettin' awful careless, ain't you, hoss?" Lucas remarked dryly. He stooped over Sarah's limp form and withdrew the knife with a casual wrench.

"More'n likely he's chicken-hearted about killing womenfolk," Andy sneered, emerging from the darkness.

Lowering his still poised knife, Travis stalked forward. "That was senseless," he said, burning with rage. "I could have silenced her with my hilt."

"Supposin' you'd have missed at that distance?" Lucas drawled, wiping the blade clean on Sarah's dress.

"What's this fuss about a squaw, anyhow?" Andy added.

"She was white, dammit," Travis said sharply.

"Maybe once," Lucas agreed, taking one of Sarah's arms. "But she done been too long with the Comanches." He dragged the body inside the tepee.

"She told me where to find Evelyn."

"Then she served her purpose," Andy said indifferently.

Travis saw the futility of pursuing the incident and returned to the matter at hand. "What are you two doing here, anyway?"

"We heard some Mes-cans talkin'," Lucas said, stepping out of the tepee, "and figured to go after somethin' more valuable than furs."

"Guns," Andy clarified. "Repeating rifles to be exact."

"Seems Ramon Segara brung a

221

couple waggons just full of 'em," Lucas continued. "Traders in Santa Fe would pay a right nice penny."

"Segara bought Evelyn," Travis said. "He's holding her in a lodge on down a ways." He nodded the direction.

"That oughta be where we'll find the guns and waggons," Lucas said, looking off.

"What're we a-standin' here for?" Andy said cheerfully. "Let's go fetch your gal, and git rich at the same time!"

15

WHILE the Wallers crouched behind one of the three waggons and kept eagle eyes on the four men drinking and talking around a campfire, their voices becoming more boisterous as the tequila bottle continually changed hands, Travis belly-snaked to the rear of the huge tepee. It had been agreed that he would be allowed to get Evelyn out of harm's way before they braced the guards, and Travis only hoped greed would not goad the brothers into action ahead of time.

Reaching the lodge, Travis drew himself to his knees and keenly listened for stirrings inside. There was only silence but it did not guarantee that Evelyn was alone. He couldn't chance calling to her and would have to trust that she made no startled cry upon his unorthodox entrance.

The outside hide covering parted easily under the sharp knife with scarcely a sound and Travis mentally cursed on seeing there was still the inner liner blocking his way. No voice or gunshot challenged his intent. He plunged the blade into the hide and severed it with a quick downward movement. This time he heard a woman's gasp and hurriedly shoved his head inside.

"Evelyn, it's Travis," he said in a loud whisper. "Don't scream!"

"Travis . . . " a small, familiar voice repeated in a relieved, half-sobbing gasp.

Travis crawled through the opening and started toward Evelyn's dark, huddled shape on the far side of the rear of the tepee. There was no fire to guide him and the light from the smoke hole fell on the opposite side of the enclosure. Then he was beside her and she thrust her bound body up into his arms, pressing her soft, tear-streaked face against his rough, stubbled cheek. His dry lips found her trembling mouth and muffled her mindless words of love.

For a space of time Travis held Evelyn possessively in his comforting arms, but all too soon the guards' laughter and drunken voices reminded him of the danger that lay outside. His hands had already traced some of the many thong loops burrowing into Evelyn's flesh and dress, and he was fearful of using the knife in the darkness. It would take time to pick loose the intricate knots — and time was running out. The Waller boys weren't going to sit patiently too much longer. Even when freed, Evelyn would need time to recover the use of her limbs after being tied so long. He'd best carry her out to safety and then see to her bonds.

Travis started to gently gather Evelyn up into his arms when suddenly jingling footsteps shambled to the lodge. He released her and barely had time to press back into the deeper shadows before the entrance flap flew open and a brawny *vaquero* lurched inside.

Framed by the light from outside that bisected almost the full length of the enclosure, he stood allowing his eyes to adjust to the gloom. Lust and courage prodded by liquor, he staggered toward Evelyn, whose tied, moccasined feet were visible in the light. His slurred words of Spanish needed no translation as to his intent, and outside the men hooted and carried on, praising his bravery and speculating on Segara's wrath. Spurs almost muffled by the thick furs and blankets, the man was almost to Evelyn when a sliver of light filtering through the ripped inner liner and outer covering caught and held his attention.

"*Qué pasa?*" he exclaimed, shaking off some of his drunkenness and becoming suddenly alert.

Knife thrusting, Travis came at him out of the darkness. The *vaquero* heard and saw his movement and twisted toward him, thwarting the intended kill. The blade scraped along the man's ribs, digging flesh and bringing a pained howl and halting his hand fumbling for the holstered six-gun. He grabbed Travis' wrist in both hands and they reeled about wildly.

Evelyn lay awkwardly on her back, head raised, large eyes intent on the men's struggling, panting silhouettes careening back and forth from dim light into dark shadows. Her lithe muscles twisted and contracted against the confining rawhide as she vainly sought to free herself and aid Travis. She was aware of a tumult outside, but her concentration remained on the brutal contest playing out before her. The knife fell, and the men began mauling each other with vicious, meaty blows that, in the darkness, reminded her of butcher shop sounds and made her wish she could cover her ears.

Then they were on the ground, only their madly kicking boots fleetingly moving into the faint light. The

Mexican's big rowelled spurs glinted and jangled with his frantic motions, stabbing and shredding the ground-covering furs and blankets. The blows ceased and were replaced by the men's grunting gasps as they wrestled about. A voice began a tortured yell that abruptly ended as a neck bone broke with a sharp, savage pop. The noisy spurs continued a moment, then were silent. A man's deep, erratic breathing issued from the blackness.

Whole body tight, Evelyn waited breathlessly, straining to extend her senses and see into the darkness as the heavy breathing drew nearer. And then the fear and tension gushed from her in a long, relieved sob at the sound of Travis' soothing voice. He lifted her shoulders and again took her into his sheltering arms. Before Evelyn could find her voice a shout came from outside:

"Dixon, if'n you're alive in there, speak up — 'fore we come in blastin'!"

"No need for that, Lucas," Travis

answered. "I'm coming out with Evelyn." Careful as handling a baby, he picked up Evelyn and carried her from the dark tepee and out into the firelight.

16

THE Wallers thoughtfully dragged the three guards' knifed-up corpses away from Evelyn's 'delicate eyes', then stood listening as she told of Ramon Segara's planned invasion of Texas.

"Why as good Texans it's our patriotic duty to take them rifles and such to Santa Fe," Andy eagerly rationalised.

"And destroy what we can't tote," Lucas said with equal 'patriotic' fervour. "C'mon, Andy, they's a heap of work ahead of us." They turned and hurried off to the waggons.

"Old Sam Houston would have been right proud of those boys," Travis commented dryly, referring to the late patriarch of Texas.

"But Santa Fe is in New Mexico Territory," Evelyn said curiously, pausing in her unpleasant task of restoring feeling to her deeply rawhide-marked wrists. "Wouldn't it be simpler to destroy everything here?"

"Yeah," Travis agreed. "But not as profitable for the Wallers." Evelyn nodded somewhat sheepishly and returned her attention to her throbbing wrists. "Wait here while I go saddle us a couple of horses," Travis said and strode toward the picket line.

By the time Evelyn had recovered enough to hobble back and forth around the campfire, absently watching the Wallers' furious haste as they overloaded a waggon with only the most valuable boxes and hitched up a team of mules with the deft precision of stagecoach stock-tenders, Travis had returned with two horses bearing large Mexican saddles. He helped her mount, and it felt strange to sit a saddle after days of riding near bareback with the Comanches.

Stepping astride his horse, Travis looked to the Wallers who were sadly smashing whisky bottles over the contents of boxes they were forced to leave behind. "You fellas about finished?" he enquired.

"Just about," Andy replied. He paused to take a healthy swig from a bottle he was emptying over an open box of shiny cartridges.

Suddenly a woman's distant scream cut the night air, followed by her greatly agitated voice moving farther away, toward the Comanche village. The four tensed, exchanging tight glances, then Lucas casually commented, "Appears somebody done found that dead ol' white squaw."

"Sarah . . . ?" Evelyn gasped in surprise.

Lucas shrugged. "We wasn't introduced proper."

"Not enough time to wet everythin' down," Andy said, his eyes quickly sweeping the scattered boxes and their contents.

"Fire it up," Lucas said, putting a match to one of the cigars he'd appropriated from the dead Mexicans, "and I'll waste one of them dynamite sticks on the rest." He whirled and rushed to the wagon as sounds of the Comanche village coming to excited life reached them.

"We're making straight for the canyon," Travis said, bringing Evelyn from her mixed thoughts about old Sarah's fate. "No matter what happens — keep riding and don't stop until you're well away from here."

"Let's clear out," Andy shouted, striking a match on his teeth and setting its flame to a whisky-soaked side of the huge tepee. He bolted to the waggon, where Lucas was leaning over the seat and pawing a stick of dynamite from an open box. Travis and Evelyn galloped past as he clambered aboard, took the reins and, standing erect like a Roman chariot driver, bellowed at the already fire-spooked team. The mules threw their weight against their collars and the weight-groaning waggon lurched forward.

"Tend to the drivin'," Lucas shouted over the noise, "and I'll tend to the throwin' and shootin'." He put the red glowing cigar tip to the fuse, let it sizzle a moment, then tossed the stick back toward the strewn boxes.

Several sounds came in swift sequence. Following a whisky trail, flames from the burning tepee reached a box of cartridges and set them off like firecrackers. Then the fuse ignited the dynamite and its deafening force hurled shattered boxes high in all directions. The bunch of Comanches drawn by the fire whirled and took to their heels in mindless panic, pursued by flaming debris and more rocketing detonations.

The rumbling waggon whirled on, the mules crazed by the explosions racing at top speeds and swept past the back side of the Comanche village. Lucas let fly with another fuse-sputtering dynamite stick that arced over the top of a tepee and landed in the midst of a clustered group, bringing an even wilder uproar.

Buffalo Woman had the misfortune to be one of them, and her last mortal scream was wiped out by the ear-splitting blast that sent them all into oblivion.

On horse and foot the furious Apaches and Comanches rallied to give chase, led by their chiefs and a madly cursing Ramon Segara and most of his bandits. War cries, twanging bows, and roaring rifles and pistols filled the air as the pursuers thundered after the swaying, jolting waggon and the two galloping riders out ahead. A dynamite stick scattered those in the lead and wreaked bloody havoc amongst those behind. Wisely fanned wide, the horde raced to circle their prey and cut them off from the canyon passage.

A bullet splintered into the seat rest, prompting Lucas to take up a new Winchester from the floor and strive to aim true while the lurching waggon swayed back and forth. The rifle blared and a nearing warrior abruptly left his horse in a loose, sliding fall. Grinning and chomping his cigar, he flipped the lever rapidly, sending bullets flying as soon as a cartridge entered the chamber, and kept the screeching throng at bay. Strident yells still lashed at him from all quarters and, bracing himself in the careening waggon, Lucas strained to see beyond the bobbing heads of the runaway team.

Far in front Dixon and his girl, bodies stretched low over their wildly galloping horses' extended necks, were almost to the yawning passage which loomed closer and closer. Once the waggon entered the canyon he'd loose another stick of dynamite and close it up good, right in the Indians' faces.

"By God, Andy," Lucas shouted, laying the rifle aside and twisting in the seat to reach back over and fumble with the dynamite sticks, "I think we's a-gonna make it by the skin of our teeth." Andy was too busy calling to the terrified animals who were fighting their bits to reply.

A passing lance made an eerie swishing sound and its tip grazed the off-mule's rump, sending him lunging against his collar. Instantly the waggon slewed to the side and started whipping back and forth, jouncing both men hard and long. Rolling his big shoulders in balance to the pitch and weave, Andy urgently fought to keep the waggon on course as they charged toward the defile that Travis and Evelyn, blonde hair flying, were about to enter.

Suddenly an invisible, but potent force savagely knocked Andy off his feet and sat him down jarringly on the seat. He confusedly felt a great sense of shock as a growing numbness swept through him. Things were fast slipping away, while at the far edge of a dimming world, the racketing gunshots were running out into nothingness.

Coming up to the canyon's mouth, the overburdened vehicle again swung broadside, began to tip in its skid, and overturned with a resounding crash, flinging its cargo about like matchsticks inside a widening dust cloud. Broken waggon-tongue dragging, the crazed mules raced away from the tumbling waggon and scattered a closing group of yelling Indians. The heavy body slammed to rest on its side, littering the ground with smashed crates and their contents.

Chest crushed, lungs rapidly filling with blood, Lucas lay sprawled grotesquely amid the crates and listened to the strange silence. Then victorious war cries filled the dust-clogged air as the Indians and Mexicans pushed their horses forward. With a desperate wrenching of will Lucas managed to cling to life until Ramon Segara, Stone Eagle and Alchisay and their lot were crowding around the waggon. Then he feebly brought the fuse of the tightly held dynamite stick up to the still-glowing cigar tip jammed in a bloody corner of his mouth.

Halfway along the twisting passage, Travis and Evelyn were startled by the gigantic, echoing blast that closed

238

the way behind them and began to dislodge rocks and streams of dirt and gravel from the surrounding walls. Reins-lashing their tired horses into a turbulent run, they narrowly avoided careening rocks and spilling debris and kept ahead of the thick, blinding whirlwind of dust that raced through the towering corridor. Then they burst from the canyon and pounded out across the small valley. They hauled up at the far end and, letting their fatigued horses blow, looked back at the dust-spewing mouth of the rumbling canyon.

Slowly the tautness left Evelyn and her face softened in the luminous night. The Valley of Tears, and all that it held, was suddenly far away. It was like a bad dream which swiftly faded upon awakening. She turned to Travis, a fixed inexpressibility holding his every facial feature, who seemed to be gravely waiting for her to speak. She managed a smile through her weariness and said very steadily and surely:

"Travis, take me home to Texas."

Travis Dixon grinned, wider than he'd ever done in his entire life, and his arm went around her shoulders. She burrowed her head against his shoulder for a long moment, then they began the long ride back home.

THE END